P9-CQT-340

ANDRE NORTON

"An author who has tantalized and enthralled readers for years . . ."

—*The Saturday Review*

"A superb storyteller with a narrative pace all her own . . ."

—*The New York Times*

"Outstanding among science fiction authors . . . Expert in evoking a feeling of terror and horror . . . A master at sustained suspense."

—*The Washington Star*

"Nobody can top Miss Norton when it comes to swashbuckling science fiction adventure stories . . ."

—*The St. Louis Globe-Democrat*

Now, enter her worlds of

HIGH SORCERY

Ace Science Fiction Books by Andre Norton

BREED TO COME
CROSSROADS OF TIME
EXILES OF THE STARS
EYE OF THE MONSTER
HIGH SORCERY
ICE CROWN
IRON CAGE
KNAVE OF DREAMS
LAVENDER GREEN MAGIC
MOON OF THREE RINGS

PLAGUE SHIP
QUEST CROSSTIME
RED HART MAGIC
SECRET OF THE LOST RACE
STAR BORN
THE STARS ARE OURS!
UNCHARTED STARS
VOODOO PLANET / STAR HUNTER
VOORLOPER
THE ZERO STONE

The Forerunner *Series*

STORM OVER WARLOCK
ORDEAL IN OTHERWHERE
FORERUNNER FORAY

The Ross Murdock *Series*

THE TIME TRADERS
GALACTIC DERELICT
THE DEFIANT AGENTS
KEY OUT OF TIME

The Witch World *Series*

WITCH WORLD
WEB OF THE WITCH WORLD
YEAR OF THE UNICORN
THREE AGAINST THE WITCH
   WORLD

WARLOCK OF THE WITCH WORLD
SORCERESS OF THE WITCH
   WORLD
TREY OF SWORDS
ZARSTHOR'S BANE

ANDRE NORTON

HIGH SORCERY

ACE FANTASY BOOKS
NEW YORK

All characters in this book are fictitious.
Any resemblance to actual persons, living or dead,
is purely coincidental.

HIGH SORCERY

An Ace Fantasy Book / published by arrangement with
the author

PRINTING HISTORY
First Ace printing / March 1970
Second Ace printing / October 1971
Third Ace printing / December 1973
Fourth Ace printing / January 1976
Fifth Ace printing / March 1979
Sixth Ace printing / October 1982
Seventh Ace printing / May 1984

All rights reserved.
Copyright © 1970 by Andre Norton
Cover art by Steve Hickman
This book may not be reproduced in whole or in part,
by mimeograph or any other means, without permission.
For information address: The Berkley Publishing Group,
200 Madison Avenue, New York, N.Y. 10016.

Wizard's World, from *If*, copyright © 1967 by Galaxy Publishing Corp.
Toys of Tamisan, from *If*, copyright © 1969 by Galaxy Publishing Corp.

ISBN: 0-441-33711-2

Ace Fantasy Books are published by The Berkley Publishing Group,
200 Madison Avenue, New York, New York 10016.
PRINTED IN THE UNITED STATES OF AMERICA

CONTENTS

WIZARD'S WORLD

I

CRAIKE'S swollen feet were agony, every breath he drew fought a hot band imprisoning his laboring lungs. He clung weakly to a rough spur of rock in the canyon wall, swayed against it, raking his flesh raw on the stone. That weathered red and yellow rock was no more unyielding than the murderous wills behind him. And the stab of pain in his calves was no less than the pain of their purpose in his dazed mind.

He had been on the run so long, ever since he had left the E-Camp. But until last night—no, two nights ago—when he had given himself away at the gas station, he had not known what it was to be actually hunted. The will-to-kill which fanned from those on his trail was so intense it shocked his Esper senses, panicking him completely.

Now he was trapped in wild country, and he was city born. Water—Craike flinched at the thought of water. Espers should control their bodies, that was what he had been taught. But there come times when cravings of the flesh triumph over will.

He winced, and the spur grated against his half-naked breast. They had a "hound" on him right enough. And that brain-twisted Esper slave who fawned and served the mob masters would have no difficulty in trailing him straight to any pocket into which he might crawl. A last remnant of rebellion sent Craike reeling over the gravel of the long-dried stream bed.

Espers had once been respected for their "wild talents," then tolerated warily. Now they were used under guard for slave labor. And the day was coming soon when the fears of the normals would demand their extermination. They had been trying to prepare against that.

First they had worked openly, petitioning to be included in spaceship crews, to be chosen for colonists on the Moon and Mars; then secretly when they realized the norms had no intention of allowing that. Their last hope was flight to the waste spots of the world, those refuse places resulting from the same atomic wars which had brought about the birth of their kind.

Craike had been smuggled out of an eastern E-Camp, provided with a cover and sent to

explore the ravaged area about the onetime city
of Reno. But he had broken his cover for the
protection of a girl, only to learn, too late, that
she was bait for an Esper trap. He had driven a
stolen speeder until the last drop of fuel was
gone, and after that he had kept blindly on, running, until now.

The contact with the Esper "hound" was clear;
they must almost be in sight behind. Craike
paused. They were not going to take him alive,
wring from him knowledge of his people and
recondition him into another "hound." There
was only one way; he should have known from
the first.

His decision had shaken the "hound". Craike
bared teeth in a death's-head grin. Now the mob
would speed up. But their quarry had already
chosen a part of the canyon wall where he might
pull his tired and aching body up from one hold
to another. He moved deliberately now, knowing that, having lost hope, he could throw aside
the need for haste. He would be able to ac-
complish his purpose before they brought a gas
rifle to bear on him.

At last he stood on a ledge, the sand and gravel
some fifty feet below. For a long moment he
rested, steadying himself with both hands
braced on the stone. The weird beauty of the
desert country was a pattern of violent color
under the afternoon sun. Craike breathed slowly;
he had regained a measure of control. There
came shouts as they sighted him.

He leaned forward and, as if he were diving

into the river which had once run there, he
hurled himself outward to the clean death he
sought.

Water, water in his mouth! Dazed, he flailed
water until his head broke surface. Instinct took
over, and he swam, fought for air. The current of
the stream pulled him against a boulder collared
with froth, and he arched an arm over it, lifting
himself, to stare about in stupefied bewilderment.

He was close to one bank of a river. Where the
colorful cliff of the canyon had been there now
rolled downs thickly covered with green
growth. The baking heat of the desert had vanished; there was even a slight chill in the air.

Dumbly Craike left his rock anchorage and
paddled ashore, to lie shivering on sand while
the sun warmed his battered body. What *had*
happened? When he tried to make sense of it, the
effort hurt his mind almost as much as had the
"hound's" probe.

The Esper hound! Craike jerked up, old panic
stirring. First delicately and then urgently, he
cast a thought-seek about him. There was life in
plenty. He touched, classified and disregarded
the flickers of awareness which mingled in
confusion—animals, birds, river dwellers. But
nowhere did he meet intelligence approaching
his own. It was a wilderness world without man
as far as Esper ability could reach.

Craike relaxed. Something had happened. He
was too tired, too drained to speculate as to what.
It was enough that he was saved from the death
he had sought, that he was *here* instead of *there*.

He got stiffly to his feet. The time was the

same, he thought, late afternoon. *Shelter, food*—he set off along the stream. He found and ate berries spilling from bushes that birds had raided above him. Then squatting above a side eddy of the stream, he scooped out a fish and ate the flesh raw.

The land along the river was rising; he could see the beginning of a gorge ahead. Later, when he had climbed those heights, he caught sight through the twilight of the fires. There were four of them burning some miles to the southwest, set out in the form of a square!

Craike sent out a thought probe. Yes, men! But there was an alien touch. This was no hunting mob. And he was drawn to the security of the fires, the camp of men in the dangers of the night. Only, as Esper, he was not one with them, but an outlaw. And he dare not risk joining them.

He retraced his path to the river and holed up in a hollow not large enough to be termed a cave. Automatically he probed again for danger. He found nothing but animal life. He slept at last, drugged by exhaustion of mind and body.

The sky was gray when he roused, swung cramped arms and stretched. Craike had awakened with the need to know more of that camp. He climbed once again to the vantage point, shut his eyes to the early morning and sent out a seeking.

It was a camp of men far from home. They were not hunters, but merchants, traders. Craike located one mind among the rest and read in it the details of a bargain to come. Merchants from another country, a caravan. But a sense of separa-

tion grew stronger as the fugitive Esper sorted
out thought streams, absorbing scraps of knowledge thirstily. There was a herd of burden-
bearing animals, nowhere any indication of
machines. He sucked in a deep breath—he
was—he was in another world!

They were merchants traversing a wilderness—a wilderness? Though he had been
driven into desert the day before, the land
through which he had earlier fled could not be
termed a wilderness. It was over-populated because there was too many war-poisoned areas
where mankind could not live.

But from these strangers he gained a concept
of vast, barren territory broken only by small,
sparse, strips of cultivation. Craike hurried.
They were breaking camp, and the impression of
an unpeopled land they had given him made
him want to trail the caravan.

There was trouble: an attack. The caravan
animals stampeded. Craike received a startlingly
vivid mind picture of a hissing lizard thing he
could not identify. But it was danger on four
scaled feet. He winced at the fear in those minds
ahead. There was a vigor of mental broadcast in
these men which amazed him. Now the lizard
thing had been killed, but the pack animals were
scattered. It would take hours to find them. The
exasperation of the master trader was as strong to
Craike as if he stood before the man and heard
his outburst of complaint.

The Esper smiled slowly. Here, handed to him
by Fate, was his chance to gain the good will of
the travelers. Breaking contact with the men,
Craike cast around probe webs, as a fisher might

cast a net. He contacted one panic crazed animal and then another, he touched minds, soothed and brought to bear his training. Within moments he heard the dull thud of hooves on the mossy ground, no longer pounding in a wild gallop. A shaggy mount—neither pony nor horse of his knowledge, but like each in ways, its dull hide marked with a black stripe running from the root of shaggy mane to the base of its tail—came toward him and nickered questioningly. It fell behind Craike, to be joined by another and another, as the Esper walked on— until he led the full train of runaways.

He met the first of the caravan men within a quarter of a mile and savored the fellow's astonishment at the sight. Yet, after the first surprise the man did not appear too amazed. He was short and dark of skin, with a black beard of wiry, tightly-curled hair clipped to a point thrusting out from his chin. Leggings covered his limbs, and he wore a sleeveless jerkin laced with thongs. This was belted by a broad strap gaudy with painted designs, from which hung a cross-hilted sword and a knife almost as long. A peaked cap of silky white fur was drawn far down so that a front flap shaded his eyes, and another, longer strip brushed his shoulders.

"Many thanks, Man of Power." The words he spoke were in a clicking tongue, but Craike read their meaning mind to mind.

Then, as if puzzled on his closer examination of the Esper, the stranger frowned, his indecision slowly turning hostile.

"Outlaw! Begone, horned one!" The trader

made a queer gesture with two fingers. "We pass free from your spells—"

"Be not so quick to pass judgment, Alfric."

The newcomer was the master trader. As his man, he wore leather, but there was a gemmed clasp on his belt. His sword and knife hilt were of precious metal, as was a badge fastened to the fore of his yellow and black fur head gear.

"This one is no local outlaw." The master stood, feet apart, studying the fugitive Esper as if he were a burden pony offered as a bargain. "Would such use his power for our aid? If he is a horned one, he is unlike any I have seen."

"I am not what you think." Craike said slowly, fitting his tongue to the others' alien speech.

The master trader nodded. "That is true. And you intend us no harm; does not the sun stone so testify?" His hand went to the badge on his cap. "In this one is no evil, Alfric; rather does he come to us in aid. Have I not spoken the truth to you, stranger from the wastes?"

Craike broadcast good will as strongly as he could, and they must have been somewhat influenced by that.

"I feel—he *does* have the power!" Alfric burst forth.

"He has power," the master corrected him. "But has he striven to possess our minds as he could do? We are still our own men. No, this is no renegade Black Hood. Come."

He beckoned to Craike, and the Esper, the animals still behind him, followed into the camp where the rest of the men seized upon the ponies to adjust their packs.

The master filled a bowl from the contents of a three-legged pot set in the coals of a dying fire. Craike gulped an excellent and filling stew. When he had done, the master indicated himself.

"I am Kaluf of the Children of Noe, a far trader and trail master. Is it your will, Man of Power, to travel this road with us?"

Craike nodded. This might all be a wild dream, but he was willing to see it to its end. A day with the caravan was a chance to gather more information from the men here and should give him some inkling as to what had happened to him and where he now was.

II

Craike's day with the traders became two and then three. Esper talents were accepted by this company matter-of-factly, even asked in aid. And from the travelers he gained a picture of this world which he could not reconcile with his own.

His first impression of a large continent broken by widely separated holdings of a frontier type remained. In addition there was knowledge of a feudal government, petty lordlings holding title to lands over men of lesser birth.

Kaluf and his men had a mild contempt for their customers. Their own homeland lay to the southeast, where, in some coastal cities, they had built up an oversea trade, retaining its cream for their own consumption and peddling the rest

in the barbarous hinterland. Craike, his facility
in their click speech growing, asked questions
which the master answered freely enough.

"These inland men know no difference between Saludian silk and the weaving of the looms
in our own Kormonian quarter." He shrugged in
scorn at such ignorance. "Why should we offer
Salud when we can get Salud prices for Kormon
lengths and the buyer is satisfied? Maybe, if
these lords ever finish their private quarrels and
live at peace so that there is more travel and they
themselves come to visit in Larud or the other
cities of the Children of Noe, then shall we not
make a profit on lesser goods."

"Do these lords never try to raid your cara-
vans?"

Kaluf laughed. "They tried that once or twice.
Certainly they saw there was profit in seizing a
train and paying nothing. But we purchased trail
rights from the Black Hoods, and there was no
more trouble. How is it with you, Ka-rak? Have
you lords in your land who dare to stand against
the power of the Hooded Ones?"

Craike, taking a chance, nodded and knew he
had been right when some reserve in Kaluf vanished.

"That explains much, perhaps even why such
a man of power as you should be adrift in the
wilderness. But you need not fear in this country; your brothers hold complete rule."

A colony of Espers! Craike tensed. Had he,
through some weird chance, found here the
long-hoped-for refuge of his kind. But where
was here? His old bewilderment was lost in a
shout from the fore of the train.

"The outpost has sighted us and raised the trade banner." Kaluf quickened pace. "Within the hour we'll be at the walls of Sampur. Illif!"

Craike made for the head of the line. Sampur, by the reckoning of the train, was a city of respectable size, the domain of a Lord Ludicar, with whom Kaluf had had mutually satisfactory dealings for some time. And the master anticipated a profitable stay. But the man who had ridden out to greet them was full of news.

Racially he was unlike the traders; he was taller and longer of arm. His bare chest was a thatch of blond-red hair as thick as a bear's pelt; long braids swung across his shoulders. A leather cap, reinforced with sewn rings of metal, was crammed down over his wealth of hair, and he carried a shield slung from his saddle pad. In addition to sword and knife, he nursed a spear in the crook of his arm, from the point of which trailed a banner strip of blue stuff.

"You come in good time, Master. The Hooded Ones have proclaimed a horning, and all the out-bounders have gathered as witnesses. This is a good day for your trading, the Cloudy Ones have indeed favored you. But hurry, the Lord Ludicar is now riding in and soon there will be no good place from which to watch."

Craike fell back. Punishment? An execution? No, not quite that. He wished he dared ask questions. Certainly the picture which had leaped into Kaluf's mind at the mention of "horning" could not be true!

Caution kept the Esper aloof. Sooner or later his alien origin must be noted, though Kaluf had supplied him with a fur cap, leather jerkin, and boots from the caravan surplus.

The ceremony was to take place just outside the main gate of the stockade, which formed the outer rampart of the town. A group of braided, ring-helmed warriors hemmed in a more imposing figure with a feather plume and a blue cloak. Doubtless Lord Ludicar. Thronging at a respectful distance were the townfolk. But they were merely audience; the actors stood apart.

Craike's hands went to his head. The emotion which beat at him from that party brought the metallic taste of fear to his mouth and aroused his own memories. Then he steadied, probed. There was terror there, broadcast from two figures under guard. An impact of Esper power came from the three black-hooded men who walked behind the captives.

He used his own talent carefully, dreading to attract the attention of the men in black. The townsfolk opened an aisle in their ranks, giving free passage to the open moorland and the green stretch of forest not too far away.

Fear—in one of those bound, stumbling prisoners it was abject, the same panic which had hounded Craike into the desert. But, though the other captive had no hope, there was a thick core of defiance, a desperate desire to strike back. And something in Craike arose to answer that.

Other men, wearing black jerkins and no hoods, crowded about the prisoners. When they stepped back Craike saw that the drab clothing of the two had been torn away. Shame, blotting out fear, came from the smaller captive. And there

was no mistaking the sex of the curves that white
body displayed. It was a girl, and very young. A
violent shake of her head loosened her hair to
flow, black and long, clothing her nakedness.
Craike drew a deep breath as he had before that
plunge into the canyon. Moving quickly he
crouched behind a bush.

The Black Hoods went about their business
with dispatch, each drawing in turn certain designs and lines in the dust of the road until they
had created an intricate pattern about the feet of
the prisoners.

A chant began in which the townspeople
joined. The fear of the male captive was an almost visible cloud. But the outrage and anger of
his feminine companion grew in relation to the
chant, and Craike could sense her will battling
against that of the assembly.

The watching Esper gasped. He could not be
seeing what his eyes reported to his brain! The
man was down on all fours, his legs and arms
stretched, a mist clung to them, changed to red-
brown hide. His head lengthened oddly, horns
sprouted. No man, but an antlered stag stood
there.

And the girl?

Her transformation came more slowly. It
began and then faded. The power of the Black
Hoods held her, fastening on her the form they
visualized. She fought. But in the end a white
doe sprang down the path to the forest, the stag
leaping before her. They whipped past the bush
where Craike had gone to earth, and he was able

to see through the illusion. Not a red stag and a
white doe, but a man and woman running for
their lives, yet already knowing in their hearts
there was no hope in their flight.

Craike, hardly knowing why he did it or who
he could aid, followed, sure that mind touch
would provide him with a guide.

He had reached the murky shadow of the trees
when a sound rang from the town. At its summoning he missed a step before he realized it
was directed against those he trailed and not
himself. A hunting horn! So this world also had
its hunted and its hunters. More than ever he
determined to aid those who fled.

But it was not enough to just run blindly on the
track of stag and doe. He lacked weapons, and
his wits had not sufficed to save him in his own
world. But there he had been conditioned
against turning on his hunters, hampered,
cruelly designed from birth to accept the quarry
role. That was not true here.

Esper power—Craike licked dry lips. They
were illusions so well done they had almost enthralled him. Could illusion undo what illusion
had done? Again the call of the horn, ominous in
its clear tone, rang in his ears and set his pulses
to pounding. The fear of those who fled was a
cord, drawing him on.

But as he trotted among the trees Craike concentrated on his own illusion. It was not a white
doe he pursued but the slim, young figure he had
seen when they stripped away the clumsy stuff
which had cloaked her, before she had shaken
loose her hair veil. No doe, but a woman, she was
not racing on four hooved feet, but running free

on two, her hair blowing behind her. No doe, but a maid!

In that moment, as he constructed that picture clearly, he contacted her in thought. It was like being washed by sea-spray, cool, remote and very clean. And, as spray, the contact vanished in an instant, only to return.

"Who are you?"

"One who follows," he answered, holding to his picture of the running girl.

"Follow no more, you have done what was needful." There was a burst of joy, so overwhelming a release from terror that it halted him. Then the cord between them broke.

Frantically Craike cast about seeking contact. There was only a dead wall. Lost, he put out a hand to the rough bark of the nearest tree. Wood things lurked here, then only did his mind touch. What did he do now?

His decision was made for him. He picked up a wave of panic again, spreading terror. But this was the fear of feathered and furred things. It came to him as ripples might run on a pool.

Fire! He caught the thought distorted by bird and beast mind. The fire leaped from tree crown, cutting a gash across the forest. Craike started on, taking the way west, away from the menace.

Once he called out as a deer flashed by him, only to know in the same moment that this was no illusion but an animal. Small creatures tunneled through the grass. A dog fox trotted and spared him a measuring gaze from slit eyes. Birds whirred, and behind them was the scent of smoke.

A mountain of flesh, muscle and fur snarled

and reared to face him. But Craike had nothing to fear from any animal. He confronted the great red bear until it whined, shuffled its feet and plodded on. More and more creatures crossed his path or ran beside him for a space.

It was their instinct which brought them, and Craike, to a river. Wolves, red deer, bears, great cats, foxes and all the rest came down to the saving water. A cat spat at the flood, but leaped in to swim. Craike lingered on the bank. The smoke was thicker and more animals broke from the wood to take to the water. But the doe— where was she?

He probed, only to meet that blank. Then a spurt of flame ran up a dead sapling, advance scout of the furnace. He yelped as a floating cinder stung his skin and took to the water. But he did not cross; rather did he swim upstream, hoping to pass the flank of the fire and pick up the missing trail again.

III

Smoke cleared as Craike trod water. He was beyond the path of the fire, but not out of danger, for the current against which he had fought his way beat here through an archway of masonry. Flanking that arch were two squat towers. As an erection it was far more ambitious than anything he had seen during his brief glimpse of Sampur. Yet, as he eyed it more closely, he could see it was a ruin. There were gaps in the narrow span across the river, a green bush sprouted from the summit of the far tower.

Craike came ashore, winning his way up the steep bank by handholds of vine and bush no alert castellan would have allowed to grow. As he reached a terrace of cobbles stippled with bunches of coarse grass, a sweetish scent of decay drew him around the base of the tower to look down at a broad ledge extending into the river. Piled on it were small baskets and bowls, some so rotted that only outlines were visible. Others were new and they all were filled with moldering foodstuffs. But those who left such offerings must have known that the tower was deserted.

Puzzled, Craike went back to the building. The stone was undressed, yet the huge blocks which formed its base were fitted together with such precision that he suspected he could not force the thin blade of a pocket knife into any crack. There had been no effort of ornamentation, at any lightening of the impression of sullen, brute force.

Wood, split and insect-bored, formed a door. As he put his hand to it Craike discovered the guardian the long-ago owners of the fortress had left in possession. His hands went to his head; the blow he felt might have been physical. Out of the stronghold before him came such a wave of utter terror and dark promise as to force him back, but no farther than the edge of the paved square about the building's foundation.

Grimly he faced that challenge, knowing it for stored emotion and not the weapon of an active will. He had his own defense against such a formless enemy. Breaking a dead branch from a bush, he twisted about it wisps of the sun-

bleached grass until he had a torch of sorts. A
piece of smoldering tinder blown from the fire
gave him a light.

Craike put his shoulder to the powdery
remnants of the door, bursting it wide. Light
against dark. What lurked there was nourished
by dark, fed upon the night fears of his species.

The round room was bare except for some
crumbling sticks of wood, a series of steps jutting out from the wall to curve about and vanish
above. Craike made no move toward further exploration, holding up the torch, seeking to see
the real, not the threat of this place.

Those who had built it possessed Esper talents, and they had used that power for twisted
purposes. He read terror and despair trapped
here by the castellans' art, and horror, an abiding
fog of what his race considered evil.

Tentatively Craike began to fight. With the
torch he brought light and heat into the dark and
cold. Now he struggled to offer peace. Just as he
had pictured a girl in flight in place of the doe, so
did he now force upon those invisible clouds of
stored suffering calm and hope. The gray window slits in the stone were uncurtained to the
streaming sunlight.

Those who had set that guardian had not intended it to hold against an Esper. Once he began
the task, Craike found the opposition melting.
The terror seeped as if it sank into the floor wave
by wave. He stood in a room which smelt of
damp and, more faintly, of the rotting food piled
below its window slits; but now it was only an
empty shell.

Craike was tired, drained by his effort; and he was puzzled. Why had he fought for this? Of what importance to him was the cleansing of a ruined tower?

Though to stay here had certain advantages. It had been erected to control river traffic. Though that did not matter for the present; just now he needed food more.

He went back to the rock of offerings, treading a wary path through the disintegrating stuff. Close to the edge he came upon a clay bowl containing coarsely ground grain and, beside it, a basket of wilted leaves filled with overripe berries. He ate in gulps.

Grass made him a matted bed in the tower, and he kindled the fire. As he squatted before its flames, he sent out a questing thought. A big cat drank from the river. Craike shuddered away from that contact with blood lust. A night-hunting bird provided a trace of awareness. There were small rovers and hunters, but nothing human.

Tired though he was, Craike could not sleep. There was the restless sensation of some demand about to be made, some task waiting. From time to time he fed the fire. Toward morning he dozed, to snap awake. A night creature drinking and a screech overhead. He heard the flutter of wings echo hollowly through the tower.

Beyond was that curious blank which had fallen between him and the girl. Craike got to his feet eagerly. That blank could be traced.

Outside it was raining, and fog hung in murky

bands among the river hollows. The blank spot
veered. Craike started after it. The tower pave-
ment became a trace of old road he followed,
weaving through the fog.

There was the sour smell of old smoke. Charred wood, black muck clung to his feet. But his
guide point was now stationary as the ground
rose, studded with outcrops of rock. So Craike
came to a mesa jutting up into a steel gray sky.

He hitched his way up by way of a long-ago
slide. The rain had stopped, but there was no
hint of sun. He was unprepared for the greeting
he met as he topped the lip of a small plateau.

A violent blow on the shoulder whirled him
halfway around, and only by a finger's width did
he escape a fall. A cry echoed his, and the blank
broke. She was there.

Moving slowly, using the same technique he
knew to soothe frightened animals, Craike
raised himself again. The pain in his shoulder
was sharp when he tried to put much weight
upon his left arm. But now he saw her clearly.

She sat cross-legged, a boulder at her back, her
hair a rippling cloud of black through which her
hands and arms shown starkly white. She had
the thin, three-cornered face of a child who has
known much harshness. There was no beauty
there; the flesh had been too much worn by
spirit. Only her eyes, watchful-wary as those of a
feline, considered him bleakly. In spite of his
beam of good will, she gave him no welcome.
And she tossed another stone from hand to hand
with the ease of one who had already scored with
such a weapon.

"Who are you?" she spoke aloud.

"He who followed you." Craike fingered the bruise on his shoulder, not taking his eyes from hers.

"You are no Black Hood." It was a statement, not a question. "But you, also, have been horned." That was another statement.

Craike nodded. In his own time and place he had indeed been "horned."

Just as her thrown stone had struck without warning, so came her second attack. There was a hiss. Within striking distance a snake flickered a forked tongue.

Craike did not give ground. The snake head expanded, fur ran over it; there were legs, a plume of tail fluffed. A dog fox yapped once at the girl and vanished. Craike read her recoil, the first uncertainty.

"You have the power!"

"I have power." He corrected her.

But her attention was no longer his. She was listening to something he could hear with neither ear nor mind. Then she ran to the edge of the mesa. He followed.

On this side the country was more rolling, and across it now came mounted men moving in and out of mist pools. They rode in silence, and over them was the same blanketing of thought as the girl had used.

Craike glanced about. There were loose stones; and the girl had already proven her marksmanship with such. But they would be no answer to the weapons the others had. Flight was no solution either.

The girl sobbed once, a broken cry so unlike

the iron will she had shown that Craike started.
She leaned perilously over the drop, staring
down at the horsemen.

Then her hands moved with desperate speed.
She tore hairs from her head, twisted and snarled
them between her fingers, breathed on them,
looped them with a stone for weight, casting the
tangled mass out to land before the riders.

The mist curled and took on substance. Where
there had been only rock there was now a thicket
of thorn, so knotted that no flesh creature could
push through it. The hunters paused, then they
rode on again, but now they drove a reeling,
naked man, a man kept going by a lashing whip
whenever he faltered.

Again the girl sobbed, burying her face in her
hands. The wretched captive reached the thorn
barrier. Under his touch it melted. He stood
there, weaving drunkenly.

A whip sang. He went to his knees under its
cut; a trapped animal's wail went on the wind.
Slowly, with a blind seeking, his hands went out
to small stones about him. He gathered them,
spread them anew in patterns. The girl had
raised her head, watching dry-eyed, but seething
with hate and the need to strike back. But she did
not move.

Craike dared lay a hand on her narrow shoulder, feeling through her hair the chill of her skin,
while the hair itself clung to his fingers as if it
had the will to smother and imprison. He tried to
pull her away, but he could not move her.

The naked man crouched in the midst of his
pattern, and now he chanted, a compelling call

the girl could not withstand. She wrenched free
of Craike's hold. But as she went she spared a
thought for the man who had tried to save her.
She struck out, her fist landing on the stone
bruise. Pain sent him reeling back as she went
over to the rim of the mesa, her face a mask
which no friend nor enemy might read. But there
was no resignation in her eyes as she was forced
to the meeting below.

IV

By the time Craike reached a vantage point the
girl stood in the center of the stone ring. Outside
crouched the man, his head on his knees. She
looked down at him, no emotion showing on her
wan face. Then she dropped her hand on his
thatch of wild hair. He jerked under that touch as
he had under the whip which had printed the
scarlet weals across his back and loins. But he
raised his head, and from his throat came a
beast's mournful howl. At her gesture he was
quiet, edging closer to her as if seeking some
easement of his suffering.

The Black Hood drew in. Craike's probe could
make nothing of them. But they could not hide
their emotions as well as they concealed their
thoughts. The Esper recoiled from the avid blood
lust which lapped at the two by the cliff.

A semicircle of the black jerkined retainers
moved, too. The man who had led them lay on
the earth now, moaning softly, but the girl faced
them, head unbowed. Craike wanted to aid her.

Had he time to climb down the cliff? Clenching his teeth against the pain movement brought to his shoulder, the Esper went back, holding a mind shield as a frail protection.

Directly before him now was one of the guards. His mount caught Craike's scent, stirred uneasily, until the quieting thought of the Esper held it steady. Craike had never been forced into such action as he had these past few days. He had no real plan now; it must depend upon chance and fortune.

As if the force of her enemies' wills had slammed her back against the rock, the girl was braced by the cliff wall, a black and white figure.

Mist swirled, took on half substance of a monstrous form, was swept away in an instant. A clump of dried grass broke into flame, sending the ponies stamping and snorting. It was gone, leaving a black smudge on the earth. Illusions, realities—Craike watched. This was so far beyond his own experience that he could hardly comprehend the lightning moves of mind against mind. But he sensed these others could beat down the girl's resistance at any moment they desired, that her last futile struggles were being relished by those who decreed this as part of her punishment.

And Craike, who had believed that he could never hate more than he had when he had been touched by the fawning "hound" of the mob, was filled with a rage tempered into a chill of steel determination.

The girl went to her knees, still clutching her

hair about her, facing her tormentors with her still-held defiance. Now the man who had wrought the magic which had drawn her there crawled, all humanity gone out of him, wriggling on his belly back to his captors.

Two of the guards jerked him up. He hung limp in their hands, his mouth open in an idiot's grin. Callously, as he might tread upon a worm, the nearest Black Hood waved a hand. A metal ax flashed, and there came the dull sound of cracking bone. The guards pitched the body from them so that the bloodied head almost touched the girl.

She writhed a last frenzied attempt to break the force which pinned her. Without haste the guards advanced. One caught at her hair, pulling it tautly from her head.

Craike shivered. The thrill of her agony reached him. This was what she feared most and had fought so long to prevent. If ever, he must move now. And that part of his brain which had been feverishly seeking a plan went into action.

Ponies pawed, reared and went wild with panic. One of the Black Hoods swung around to face the terrorized animals. But his own mount struck out with teeth and hooves. Guardsmen shouted, and above their cries arose the shrill squeals of the animals.

Craike stood his ground, keeping the ponies in terror-stricken revolt. The guard who held the handful of hair slashed at the tress with a knife, severing it at a palm's distance away from her head. But in the same moment she moved. The knife leaped free from the man's grasp, while the severed hair twined itself about his hands, binding them until the blade buried itself in his throat and he went down.

One of the Black Hoods was also finished, tramped into a feebly squirming thing by the ponies. Then from the ground burst a sheet of flame which split into balls, drifting through the air or rolling along the earth.

The Esper wet his lips; that was not his doing. He did not have to feed the panic of the animals now; they were truly mad. The girl was on her feet. Before his thought could reach her she was gone, swallowed up in a mist which arose to blanket the fire balls. Once more she cut their contact; there was a blank void where she had been.

Now the fog thickened. Through it came one of the ponies, foam dripping from its blunt muzzle. It bore down on Craike, eyes gleaming red through a tangled forelock. With a scream it reared.

Craike's hand grabbed a handful of mane as he leaped, avoiding teeth and hooves. Then, somehow, he gained the pad saddle, locking his fingers in the coarse hair, striving to hold his seat against the bucking, enraged beast. It broke into a run, and the Esper plastered himself to the heaving body. For the moment he made no attempt at mind control.

Behind, the Black Hoods came out of their stunned bewilderment. They were questing feverishly, and he had to concentrate on holding his shield against them. A pony fleeing in terror would not excite them; a pony under control would provide them with a target.

Later he could circle about and try to pick up the trail of the witch girl. Flushed with success, Craike was sure he could provide her with a rear guard no Black Hood could pass.

The fog was thick, and the pace of the pony began to slacken. Once or twice it bucked half-heartedly, giving up when it could not dislodge its rider. Craike drew his fingers in slow, soothing sweeps down the sweating curve of its neck.

There were no more trees about, and the unshod hooves pounded on sand. They were in a dried water course, and Craike did not try to turn from that path. Then his luck ran out.

What he had ignorantly supposed to be a rock ahead, heaved up seven feet or more. A red mouth opened in a great roar. He had believed the bear he had seen fleeing the fire to be a giant, but this one was a nightmare monster.

The pony screamed with an almost human note of despair and whirled. Craike gripped the mane and tried to mind control the bear. But his surprise had lasted seconds too long. A vast clawed paw struck, ripping across pony hide and human thigh. Then Craike could only cling to the running mount.

How long he was able to keep his seat he never knew. Then he slipped; there was a throb of pain as he struck the ground; it was followed by blackness.

It was dusk when he opened his eyes, fighting agony in his head and his leg. But later there was moonlight. And that silver-white spotlighted a waiting shape. Green slits of eyes regarded him remotely. Dizzily he made contact.

A wolf, hungry, yet with a wariness which recognized in the prone man an enemy. Craike fought for control. The wolf whined. Then it arose, its prick ears sharp-cut in the moonlight, its nose questing for the scent of other, less disturbing prey; and it was gone.

Craike edged up against a boulder and sorted out sounds. There was a rush of water. He moved a paper-dry tongue over cracked lips. There would be water to drink, to wash his wounds, water!

With a groan Craike worked his way to his feet, holding fast to the top of the rock when his torn leg threatened to buckle under him. The same inner drive which had kept him going through the desert brought him down to the river.

By sunrise he was seeking a shelter, wanting to lie up, as might the wolf, in some secret cave until his wounds healed. All chance of finding the witch girl was lost. But as he crawled along the shingle, leaning on a staff he had found in drift wood, he kept alert for any trace of the Black Hoods.

It was mid-morning on the second day that his snail's progress brought him to the river towers; and it took another hour for him to reach the terrace. Gaunt and worn, his empty stomach complaining, he wanted nothing more than to sink down in the nest of grass he had gathered and cease to struggle.

Perhaps he might have done so had not a click-clack of sound from the river put him on the defensive; his staff was now a club. These were not Black Hoods, but farmers, local men bound for the market of Sampur with products from their fields. They had paused and were making a choice among the least appetizing of their wares for a tribute to be offered to the tower demon.

Craike hitched stiffly to a point where he could witness that sacrifice. But when he assessed the contents of their dugout, the heaping basket piled between the paddlers, his hunger took command.

Fob off a demon with a handful of meal and a too-ripe melon would they? There were three haunches of cured meat and other stuff on board.

Craike voiced a roar which could have done credit to the red bear, a roar which altered into a demand for meat. The paddlers nearly lost control of their crude craft. But one reached for a haunch and threw it blindly on the refuse-covered rock, while his companion added a basket of small cakes into the bargain.

"Enough, little men," Craike's voice boomed hollowly. "You may pass free."

They needed no urging; they did not look at those threatening towers as their paddles bit into the water, adding impetus to the pull of the current.

Craike watched them well out of sight before he made a slow descent to the rock. The effort he was forced to expend warned him that a second such trip might be impossible, and he inched back to the terrace dragging both meat and cakes.

The cured haunch he worried into strips, using his pocket knife. It was tough, not too pleasant to the taste and unsalted. But he found it more appetizing than the cakes of baked meal. With this supply he could afford to lie up and favor his leg.

About the claw rents the flesh was red and puffed. Craike had no dressing but river water and the leaves he had tied over the tears. Sampur was beyond his power to reach, and to contact men traveling on the river would only bring the Black Hoods.

He lay in his grass nest and tried to sort out the events of the past few days. This was a land in which Esper powers were allowed free range. He had no idea of how he had come here, but it seemed to his feverish mind that he had been granted another chance—one in which the scales of justice were more balanced in his favor. If he could only find the girl, learn from her—

Tentatively, without real hope, he sent out a questing thought. Nothing. He moved impatiently, wrenching his leg, so that his head swam with pain. His throat and mouth were dry. The lap of water sounded in his ears. He was thirsty again, but he could not crawl down slope and up once more. Craike closed his eyes wearily.

V

Craike's memory of the hours which followed thereafter was dim. Had he seen a demon in the doorway? A slavering wolf? A red bear?

Then the girl sat there, cross-legged as he had seen her on the mesa, her cloak of hair about her. A hand emerged from the cloak to lay wood on the fire. Illusions?

But would an illusion turn to him, put firm, cool fingers upon his wound, somehow driving out by touch the pain and fire which burned there? Would an illusion raise his head, cradling it against her so that the soft silk of her hair lay against his cheek and throat, urging on him liquid out of a crude bowl? Would an illusion sing softly to herself while she drew a fish-bone comb back and forth through her hair, until the song and the sweep of the comb lulled him into a sleep so deep that no dream walked there?

He awoke clear headed. Yet that last illusion lingered. She came from the sun-drenched world without, a bowl of fruit in her hand. For a long moment she stood gazing at him search-ingly. But when he tried mind contact, he met that wall. It was not unheeding, but a refusal to answer.

Her hair was now braided. But about her face the lock which the guardsman had shorn made an untidy fringe. Around her thin body was a strip of hide, purposefully arranged to mask all femininity.

"So," Craike spoke rustily, "you are real."

She did not smile. "I am real. You no longer dream with fever."

"Who are you?" He asked the first of his long hoarded questions.

"I am Takya." She added nothing to that.

"You are Takya, and you are a witch."

"I am Takya, and I have the power." It was an assertion of fact rather than agreement.

She settled in her favorite cross-legged posi-tion, selected a fruit from her bowl and examined it with the interest of a housewife who

has shopped for supplies on a limited budget.
Then she placed it in his hand before she chose
another for herself. He bit into the plumlike
globe. If she would only drop her barrier, let him
communicate in the way which was fuller and
deeper than speech.

"You also have the power."

Craike decided to be no more communicative
than she. He replied to that with a curt nod.

"Yet you have not been horned."

"Not as you have been. But in my own world,
yes."

"Your world?" Her eyes held some of the feral
glow of a hunting cat's. "What world, and why
were you horned there, man of sand and ash
power?"

Without knowing why Craike related the
events of the days past. Takya listened, he was
certain, with more than ears alone. She picked
up a stick from the pile of firewood and drew
patterns in the sand and ash, patterns which had
something to do with her listening.

"Your power was great enough to break a
world wall." She snapped the stick between two
fingers, threw it into the flames.

"A world wall?"

"We of the power have long known that different worlds lie together in such a fashion." She
held up her hand with the fingers tight lying one
to another. "Sometimes there comes a moment
when two touch so closely that the power can
carry one through, if at that moment there is a
desperate need for escape. But those places of
meeting cannot be readily found, and the mo-

ment of their touch can lay only for an instant.
Have you in your world no reports of men and
women who have vanished almost in sight of
their fellows?''

Remembering old tales, he nodded.
"I have seen a summoning from another
world," she continued with a shiver, running
both hands down the length of her braids as if so
she evoked a shield for both mind and body. "To
summon so is a great evil, for no man can hold in
check the power of something alien. You broke
the will of the Black Hoods when I was a beast
running from their hunt. When I made the ser-
pent to warn you off, you changed it into a fox.
And when the Black Hoods would have shorn
my power—" she looped the braids about her
wrists, caressing, treasuring them against her
small breasts, "again you broke their hold and
set me free for a second time. But this you could
not have done had you been born into this world,
for our power must follow set laws. Yours lies
outside our patterns and can cut across those
laws, even as the knife cut this." She touched the
rough patch of hair at her temple.
"Follow patterns? Then it was those patterns
in stone which drew you down from the mesa?''
"Yes. Takyi, my womb brother, whom they
slew there, was blood of my blood, bone of my
bone. When they crushed him, then they could
use him to draw me, and I could not resist. But
in the slaying of his husk they freed me, to their
great torment as Tousuth shall discover in time.''
"Tell me of this country. Who are the Black

Hoods and why did they horn you? Are you not of their breed since you have the power?"

But Tayka did not answer at once in words. Nor did she, as he had hoped, lower her mind barrier.

Her fingers now held one long hair she had pulled from her head, and this she began to weave in and out, swiftly, intricately, in a complicated series of loops and crossed strands. After a moment Craike did not see the white fingers, nor the black hair they passed in loops from one to another. Rather did he see the pictures she wrought in her weaving.

There was a wide land, largely wilderness. The impressions he had gathered from Kaluf and the traders crystallized into vivid life. Small holdings here and there were ruled by petty lords; new settlements were carved out by a scattered people moving up from the south in great wheeled wains, bringing flocks and herds and their carefully treasured seed. They stopped here and there for a season to sow and reap, until they decided upon a site for their final rooting. Tiny city-states were protected by the Black Hoods, the Espers who purposefully interbred their own gifted stock, keeping their children apart.

Takya and her brother came; such sometimes, if rarely, came from the common people. They were carefully watched by the Black Hoods, then discovered to be a new mutation, condemned as such to be used for experimentation. But for a while they were protected by the local lord who wanted Takya.

But he might not take her unwilling. The power that was hers as a virgin was wholly rift from her should she be forced, and he had wanted that power obedient to him, as a check upon the monopoly of the Black Hoods. So with some patience he had set himself to a peaceful wooing. But the Black Hoods had moved first.

Had they accomplished her taking, the end they had intended for her was not as easy as death. She wove a picture of it, with all its degradation and shame stark and open, for Craike's seeing.

"Then the Hooded Ones are evil?"

"Not wholly." She untwisted the hair and put it with care into the fire. "They do much good, and without them people would suffer. But I, Takya, am different. And after me, when I mate, there will be others also different; how different we are not yet sure. The Hooded Ones want no change; by their thinking that means disaster. So they would use me to their own purposes. Only I, Takya, shall not be so used!"

"No, you shall not." The vehemence of his own outburst startled him. Craike wanted nothing so much at that moment than to come to grips with the Black Hoods, who had planned this systematic hunt.

"What will you do now?" he asked more calmly, wishing she would share her thoughts with him.

"This is a strong place. Did you cleanse it?"

He nodded impatiently.

"So I thought. That was also a task one born to this world might not have performed. But those who pass are not yet aware of the cleansing. They will not trouble us, but pay tribute."

Craike found her complacency irritating. To lie up here and live on the offerings of river travelers did not appeal to him.

"This stone piling is older work than Sampur and much better," she continued. "It must have been a fortress for some of those forgotten ones who held lands and then vanished long before we came from the south. If it is repaired no lord of this district would have so good a roof."

"Two of us to rebuild it?" he laughed.

"Two of us, working thus."

A block of stone, the size of a brick, which had fallen from the sill of one of the needle-narrow windows, arose slowly in the air and settled into the space from which it had tumbled. Was it illusion or reality? Craike got to his feet and lurched to the window. His hand fell upon the stone which moved easily in his grasp. He took it out, weighed it, and then gently returned it to its place. This was not illusion.

"But illusion, too—if need be." There was, for the first time, a warm note of amusement in her tone. "Look on your tower, river lord!"

He limped to the door. Outside it was warm and sunny, but it was a site of ruins. Then the picture changed. Brown drifts of grass vanished from the terrace; the fallen stone was all in place. A hard-faced sentry stood wary-eyed on a repaired river arch. Another guardsman led out ponies, saddle-padded and ready; other men were about garrison tasks.

Craike grinned. The sentry on the arch lost his

helm, his jerkin. He now wore the tight tunic of
the Security Police; his spear was a gas rifle. The
ponies misted, and in their place a speedster sat
on the stone. He heard her laugh.

"Your guard, your traveling machine. But
how grim, ugly. This is better!"

Guards, machine, all were swept away. Craike
caught his breath at the sight of delicate winged
creatures dancing in the air, displaying a joy of
life he had never known. Fawns, little people of
the wild, came to mingle with shapes of such
beauty and desire that at last he turned his head
away.

"Illusion." Her voice was hard and mocking.

But Craike could not believe that what he had
seen had been born from hardness and mockery.

"All illusions. We shall be better now with
warriors. As for plans, can you suggest any better
than to remain here and take what fortune sends,
for a space?"

"Those winged dancers—where?"

"Illusions!" she returned harshly. "But such
games tire one. I do not think we shall conjure up
any garrison before they are needed. Come, do
not tear open those wounds of yours anew, for
healing is no illusion and drains one even more
of the power."

The clawed furrows were healing cleanly,
though he would bear their scars for life. He
hobbled back to the grass bed and dropped upon
it, but regretted the erasure of the sprites she had
shown him.

Once he was safely in place, Takya left with
the curt explanation that she had things to do.

But Craike was restless, too much so to remain long inside the tower. He waited until she had gone and then, with the aid of his staff, climbed to the end of the span above the river. From here the twin tower on the other bank looked the same as the one from which he had come. Whether it was also haunted Craike did not know. But, as he looked about he could see the sense of Takya's suggestion. A few illusion sentries would discourage any ordinary intrusion.

Takya's housekeeping had changed the rock of offerings. All the rotten debris was gone and none of the odor of decay now offended the nostrils at a change of wind. But at best it was a most uncertain source of supply. There could not be too many farms up river, nor too many travelers taking the waterway.

As if to refute that, his Esper sense brought him sudden warning of strangers beyond the upper bend. But, Craike tensed, these were no peasants bound for the market at Sampur. Fear, pain, anger—such emotions heralded their coming. There were three, and one was hurt. But they were not Esper; nor did they serve the Black Hoods, though they were, or had been, fighting men.

A brutal journey over the mountains where they had lost comrades, the finding of this river, the theft of the dugout they now used so expertly—it was all there for him to read. And beneath that there was something else, which, when he found it, gave Craike a quick decision in their favor—a deep hatred of the Black Hoods! They were outlaws, very close to despair, keep-

ing on a hopeless trail because it was not in them
to surrender.

Craike contacted them subtly. They must not
think they were heading into an Esper trap. He
would plant a little hope, a faint suggestion that
there was a safe camping place ahead; that was
all he could do at present. But so he drew them
on.

"No!" A ruthless order cut across his line of
contact, striking at the delicate thread with
which he was playing the strangers in. But
Craike stood firm. "Yes, yes, and yes!"

He was on guard instantly. Takya, mistress of
illusion as she had proved herself to be, might
act. But surprisingly she did not. The dugout
came into view, carried more by the current than
the efforts of its crew. One lay full length in the
bottom, while the bow paddler had slumped
forward. But the man in the stern was bringing
them in. And Craike strengthened his invisible,
unheard invitation to urge him on.

VI

Takya had not yet begun to fight. As the dugout swung toward the offering ledge one of the
Black Hoods' guardsmen appeared there, his
drawn sword taking fire from the sun. The fugitive steersman faltered until the current drew his
craft on. Craike caught the full force of the
stranger's despair, all the keener for the hope of
moments before. The Esper's irritation against
Takya flared into anger.

He made the illusion reel back, hands clutching at his breast from which protruded the shaft of an arrow. Craike had seen no bows here, but it was a weapon to suit his world. This should prove to Takya he meant what he had said.

The steersman was hidden as the dugout passed under the arch. There was a scrap of beach, the same to which Craike had swum on his first coming. He urged the man to that, beaming good will.

But the paddler was almost done, and neither of his companions could aid him. He drove the crude craft to the bank, and its bow grated on the rough gravel. Then he crawled over the bodies of the other two and fell rather than jumped ashore, turning to pull up the canoe as best he could. Craike started down. But he might have known that Takya was not so easily defeated. Though they maintained an alliance of sorts she accepted no order from him.

A brand was teleported from the tower fire, striking spearwise in the dry brush along the slope. Craike's mouth set. He tried no more arguments. They had already tested power against power, and he was willing to so battle again. But this was not the time. However, the fire was no illusion, and he could not fight it, crippled as he was. Or could he?

It was not spreading too fast, though Takya might spur it by the forces at her command. Now, there was just the spot! Craike steadied himself against a mound of fallen masonry and swept out his staff, dislodging a boulder and a shower of gravel. He had guessed right. The stone rolled to crush out the brand, and the gravel he continued to push after it smothered the creeping flames.

Red tongues dashed spitefully high in a sheet of flame, and Craike laughed. *That* was illusion; she was angry. He produced a giant pail in the air, tilted it forward, splashed its contents into the heart of that conflagration. He felt the lash of her rage, standing under it unmoved. So might she bring her own breed to heel, but she would learn he was not of that ilk.

"Holla!" That call was no illusion; it begged help.

Craike picked a careful path down slope until he saw the dugout and the man who had landed it. The Esper waved an invitation and at his summons the fugitive covered the distance between them.

He was a big man of the same brawny race as those of Sampur, his braids of reddish hair hanging well below his wide shoulders. There was the raw line of a half-healed wound down the angle of his jaw, and his sunken eyes were very tired. For a moment he stood downslope from Craike, his hands on his hips, his head back, measuring the Esper with the shrewdness of a canny officer who had long known how to judge and handle raw levies.

"I am Jorik of the Eagles' Tower." The statement was made with the same confidence as the announcement of rank from one of the petty lords. "Though"—he shrugged—"the Eagles' Tower stands no more with one stone upon the other. You have a stout lair here"—he hesitated before he concluded—"friend."

"I am Craike," the Esper answered as simply,

"and I am also one who has run from enemies. This lair is an old one, though still useful."

"Might the enemies from whom you run wear black hoods?" countered Jorik. "It seems to me that things I have just seen here have the stink of that about them."

"You are right; I am no friend to the Black Hoods."

"But you have the power."

"I have power," Craike tried to make the distinction clear. "You are welcome, Jorik. So all are welcome here who are no friends to Black Hoods."

The big warrior shrugged. "We can no longer run. If the time has come to make a last stand, this is as good a place as any. My men are done." He glanced back at the two in the dugout. "They are good men, but we were pressed when they caught us in the upper pass. Once there were twenty hands of us," he held up his fist and spread the fingers wide for counting. "They drew us out of the tower with their sorcerers' tricks, and then put us to the hunt."

"Why did they wish to make an end to you?"

Jorik laughed shortly. "They dislike those who will not fit into their neat patterns. We are free mountain men, and no Black Hood helped us win the Eagles' Tower; none aided us to hunt. When we took our furs down to the valley, they wanted to levy tribute. But what spell of theirs trapped the beasts in our deadfalls or brought them to our spears? We pay not for what we have not bought. Neither would we have made war on them. Only, when we spoke out and said it so, there were others who were encouraged to do likewise, and the Black Hoods must put an end to us before their rule was broken. So they did."

"But they did not get all of you," Craike pointed out. "Can you bring your men up to the tower? I have been hurt and can not walk without support or I would lend you a hand."

"We will come." Jorik returned to the dugout. Water was splashed vigorously into the face of the man in the bow, arousing him to crawl ashore. Then the leader of the fugitives swung the third man out of the craft and over his shoulder in a practiced carry.

When Craike had seen the unconscious man established on his own grass bed, he stirred up the fire and set out food. Jorik returned to the dugout to bring in their gear.

Neither of the other men were of the same size as their leader. The one who lay limp, his breath fluttering between his slack lips, was young, hardly out of boyhood, his thin frame showing bones rather than muscled flesh under the rags of clothing. The other was short, dark skinned and akin by race to Kaluf's men, his jaw sprouting a curly beard. He measured Craike with suspicious glances from beneath lowered red lids, turning that study to the walls about him and the unknown reaches at the head of the stair.

Craike did not try mind touch. These men were rightly suspicious of Esper arts. But he did attempt to reach Takya, only to meet the nothingness with which she cloaked her actions. Craike was disturbed. Surely now that she was convinced he was determined to give harborage to the fugitives, she would not oppose him. They had nothing to fear from Jorik and his men, but rather would gain by joining forces.

Until his wounds were entirely healed, he could not go far. And without weapons they would have to rely solely upon Esper powers for defense. Having witnessed the efficiency of the Hooded Ones' attack, Craike doubted a victory in any engagement to which those masters came fully prepared. He had managed to upset their spells merely because they had not known of his existence. But the next time he would have no such advantage.

On the other hand the tower could be defended by force of arms, bows. Craike savored the idea of archers giving a hooded force a devastating surprise. The traders had had no such arms, as sophisticated as they were, and he had seen none among the warriors of Sampur. He'd have to ask Jorik if such were known.

In the meantime he sat among his guests, watching Jorik feed the semiconscious boy with soft fruit pulp and the other man wolf down dried meat. When the latter had done, he hitched himself closer to the fire and jerked a thumb at his chest.

"Zackuth," he identified himself.

"From Larud?" Craike named the only city of Kaluf's people he could remember.

The dark man's momentary surprise had no element of suspicion. "What do you know of the Children of Noe, stranger?"

"I journeyed the plains with one called Kaluf,
a master trader of Larud."

"A fat man who laughs much and wears a
falcon plume in his cap?"

"Not so." Craike allowed a measure of chill to
ice his reply. "The Kaluf who led this caravan
was a lean man who knew the edge of a good
blade from its hilt. As for cap ornaments, he had
a red stone to the fore of his. Also he swore by the
Eyes of the Lady Lor."

Zackuth gave a great bray of laughter. "You
are no stream fish to be easily hooked, are you,
tower dweller? I am not of Larud, but I know
Kaluf, and those who travel in his company do
not wear one badge one day and another the
next. But, by the looks of you, you have fared
little better than we lately. Has Kaluf also fallen
upon evil luck?"

"I traveled safely with his caravan to the gates
of Sampur. How it fared with him thereafter I can
not tell you."

Jorik grinned and settled his patient back on
the bed. "I believe you must have parted company in haste, Lord Ka-rak?"

Craike answered that with the truth. "There
were two who were horned. I followed them to
give what aid I could."

Jorik scowled, and Zackuth spat in the fire.

"We were not horned; we have no power," the
latter remarked. "But they have other tricks to
play. So you came here?"

"I was clawed by a bear." Craike supplied a
meager portion of his adventures, "I came here
to lie up until I can heal me of that hurt."

"This is a snug hole." Jorik was appreciative. "But how got you such eating?" He popped half a fruit into his mouth and licked his juicy fingers. "This is no wilderness feeding."

"The tower is thought to be demon-haunted. Those taking passage downstream leave tribute."

Zackuth slapped his knee. "The Gods of the Waves are good to you, Lord Ka-rak, that you should stumble into such fortune. There is more than one kind of demon for haunting towers. How say you, Lord Jorik?"

"That we have also come into luck at last, since Lord Ka-rak has made us free of this hold. But perhaps you have some other thought in your head?" He spoke to the Esper.

Craike shrugged. "What the clouds decree shall fall as rain or snow," he quoted a saying of the caravan men.

It was close to sunset, and he was worried about Takya. He could not believe that she had gone permanently. And yet, if she returned, what would happen? He had been careful not to use Esper powers. Takya would have no such compunctions.

He could not analyze his feelings about her. She disturbed him, awoke emotions he refused to face. There was a certain way she had of looking sidewise. But her calm assumption of superiority pricked beneath his surface armor. The antagonism fretted against the feeling which had drawn him after her from the gates of Sampur. Once again he sent out a quest-thought and, to his surprise, it was answered.

"They must go!"

"They are outlaws, even as we. One is ill, the others worn with long running. But they stood against the Black Hoods. As such they have a claim on roof, fire and food from us."

"They are not as we!" It was again arrogance. "Send them or I shall drive them. I have the power."

"Perhaps you have the power but so do I!" He put all the assurance he could muster into that. "I tell you, no better thing could happen than for us to give these men aid; they are proven fighters."

"Swords can not stand against the power!"

Craike smiled. His plans were beginning to move even as he carried on this voiceless argument. "Not swords, no, Takya. But all fighting is not done with swords or spears. Nor with the power either. Can a Black Hood think death to his enemy when he himself is dead, killed from a distance, and not by mind power his fellows could trace and be armored against?"

He had caught her attention. She was acute enough to know that he was not playing with words, that he knew of what he spoke. Quickly he built upon that spark of interest. "Remember how your illusion guard died upon the offering rock when you would warn off these men?"

"By a small spear." She was contemptuous again.

"Not so." He shaped a picture of an arrow and then of an archer releasing it from the bow, of its speeding true across the river to strike deep into the throat of an unsuspecting Black Hood.

"You have the secret of this weapon?"

"I do. And five such arms are better than two, is that not the truth?"

She yielded a fraction. "I will return. But they will not like that."

"If you return, they will welcome you. These are no hunters of witch maidens—" he began, only to be disconcerted by her obvious amusement. Somehow he had lost his short advantage over her, yet she did not break contact.

"Ka-rak, you are very foolish. No, these will not try to mate with me, not even if I willed it so, as you will see. Does the eagle mate with the hunting cat? But they will be slow to trust me, I think. However, your plan has possibilities, and we shall see."

VII

Takya had been right about her reception by the fugitives. They knew her for what she was, and only Craike's acceptance of her kept them in the tower. That and the fact, which Jorik did not try to disguise, that they could not hope to go much farther on their own. But their fears were partly allayed when she took over the nursing of the sick youngster, using on him the same healing power she had produced for Craike's wound. By the next day she was feeding him broth and demanding service from the others as if they had been her liegemen from birth.

The sun was well up when Jorik came in whistling from a dip in the river.

"This is a stout stronghold, Lord Ka-rak. And with the power aiding us to hold it, we are not likely to be shaken out in a hurry. Doubly is that true if the lady aids us."

Takya laughed. She sat in the shaft of light from one of the narrow windows, combing her hair. Now she looked over her shoulder at them with something approaching a pert archness. In that moment she was more akin to the women Craike had known in his own world.

"Let us first see how the Lord Ka-rak proposes to defend us." There was mockery in that, enough to sting, as well as a demand that he make good his promise of the night before.

But Craike was prepared. He discarded his staff for a hold on Jorik's shoulder, while Zac-kuth slogged behind. They climbed into the forest. Craike had never fashioned a bow, and he did not doubt that his first attempts might be failures. But, as the three made their slow progress, he explained what they must look for and the kind of weapon he wanted to produce. They returned within the hour with an assortment of wood lengths with which to experiment.

After noon Zackuth grew restless and went off, to come back with a deer; he was visibly proud of his hunting skill. Craike saw bowstrings where the others saw meat and hide for the refashioning of footwear. For the rest of the day they worked with a will. It was Takya who had the skill necessary for the feathering of the arrows after Zackuth netted two black river birds.

Four days later the tower community had taken on the aspect of a real stronghold. Many of

the fallen stones were back in the walls. The two
upper rooms of the tower had been explored, and
a vast collection of ancient nests had been swept
out. Takya chose the topmost one for her own
abode and, aided by her convalescing charge,
the boy Nickus, had carried armloads of sweet-
scented grass up for both carpeting and bedding.
She did not appear to be inconvenienced by the
bats that still entered at dawn to chitter out again
at dusk. And she crooned a welcome to the
snowy owl that refused to be dislodged from a
favorite roost in the very darkest corner of the
roof.

River travel had ceased. There were no new
offerings on the rock. But Jorik and Zackuth
hunted, and Craike tended the smoking fires
which cured the extra meat against coming
need, while he worked on the bows. Shortly they
had three finished and practiced along the terrace, using blunt arrows.

Jorik had a true marksman's eye and took to
the new weapon quickly, as did Nickus. But
Zackuth was more clumsy, and Craike's stiff leg
bothered him. Takya was easily the best shot
when she would consent to try. But while
agreeing it was an excellent weapon, she pre-
ferred her own type of warfare and would sit on
the wall, braiding and rebraiding her hair with
flying fingers, to watch their shooting at marks
and applaud or jeer lightly at the results.

However, their respite was short. Craike had
the first warning of trouble. He awoke from a
dream in which he had been back in the desert

panting ahead of the mob. He awoke to discover that some malign influence filled the tower. There was a compulsion on him to get out, to flee into the forest.

He tested the silences about him tentatively. The oppression which had been in the ancient fort at his first coming had not returned; that was not it.

Someone moved restlessly in the dark.

"Lord Ka-rak?" Nickus' voice was low and hoarse, as if he struggled to keep it under control.

"What is it?"

"There is trouble—"

A bulk which could only belong to Jorik heaved up black against the faint light of the doorway.

"The hunt is up," he observed. "They move to shake us out of here like rats out of a nest."

"They did this before with you?" asked the Esper.

Jorik snorted. "Yes. It is their favorite move to battle. They would give us such a horror of our tower that we will burst forth and scatter. Then they can cut us down as they wish."

But Craike could not isolate any thought beam carrying that night terror. It seeped from the walls about them. He sent probes unsuccessfully. There was the pad of feet on the stairs, and then he heard Takya call.

"Build up the fire, foolish ones. They may discover that they do not deal with those who know nothing of them."

Flame blossomed from the coals to light a cir-

cle of sober faces. Zackuth caressed the spear
lying across his knees, but Nickus and Jorik had
eyes only for the witch maid as she knelt by the
fire, laying out some bundles of dried leaf and
fern. Her thoughts reached Craike.

"We must move or these undefended ones will
be drawn out from here as nut meats are picked
free from the shell. Give me of your power; in
this matter I must be the leader."

Though he resented anew her calm assumption of authority, Craike also recognized in it
truth. But he shrank from the task she demanded
of him. To have no control over his own Esper
arts, to allow her to use them to feed hers—it
was a violation of a kind, the very thing he
had so feared in his own world that he had
been willing to kill himself to escape it. Yet
now she asked it of him as one who had the
right!

"Forced surrender is truly evil, but given
freely in our defense it is different." Her
thoughts swiftly answered his wave of repul-
sion.

The command to flee the tower was growing
stronger. Nickus got to his feet as if dragged up.
Suddenly Zackuth made for the door, only to
have Jorik reach forth a long arm to trip him.

"You see," Takya urged, "they are already half
under the spell. Soon we shall not be able to hold
them, either by mind or body. Then they shall be
wholly lost, for ranked against us now is the high
power of the Black Hoods."

Craike watched the scuffle on the floor and
then, still reluctant and inwardly shrinking, he

limped around the fire to her side, lying down at her gesture. She threw on the fire two of her bundles of fern, and a thick, sweet smoke curled out to engulf them. Nickus coughed, put his hands uncertainly to his head and slumped, curling up as a tired child in deep slumber. And the struggle between Jorik and his man subsided as the fumes reached them.

Takya's hand was cool as it slipped beneath Craike's jerkin, resting over his heart. She was crooning some queer chant, and, though he fought to hold mind contact, there was a veil between them as tangible to his inner senses as the fern smoke was to his outer ones. For one wild second or two he seemed to see the tower room through her eyes instead of his own, and then the room was gone. He sped bodiless across the night world, casting forth as a hound on the trail.

All that had been solid in his normal sight was now without meaning. But he was able to see the dark cloud of pressure closing in on the tower and trace that back to its source, racing along the slender thread of its spinners.

There was another fire, and about it four of the Black Hoods. Here, too, was scented smoke to free minds from bodies. The essence which was Craike prowled about that fire, counting guardsmen who lay in slumber.

With an effort of will which drew heavily upon his strength, he concentrated on the staff which lay before the leader of the company, setting upon it his own commands.

It flipped up into the air, even as its master roused and clutched at it, falling into the fire.

There was a flash of blue light and a sound
which Craike felt rather than heard. The Hooded
Ones were on their feet as their master stared
straight across the flames to Craike's disembodied self. His was not an evil face; rather did it
hold elements of nobility. But the eyes were piti-
less, and Craike knew that now it was not only
war to the death between them, but war beyond
death itself. The Esper sensed that this was the
first time that the others had known of his existence, had been able to consider him as a factor
in the tangled game.

There was a flash of lightning knowledge of
each other, and then Craike was again in the
dark. He heard once more Takya's crooning and
was conscious of her touch resting above the
slow, pulsating beat of his heart.

"That was well done," her thought welcomed
him. "Now they must meet us face to face in
battle."

"They will come." He accepted the dire promise that Black Hood had made.

"They will come, but now we are more equal.
And there is not the Rod of Power to fear."

Craike tried to sit up and discovered that the
weakness born of his wounds was nothing to
that which now held him.

Takya laughed with some of her old mockery.
"Do you think you can make the Long Journey
and then romp about as a fawn, Ka-rak? Not three
days on the field of battle can equal this. Sleep
now and gather again the inner power. The end
of this venture is still far from us."

He could no longer see her face, the glimmer of
her hair veiled it, and then that shimmer reached
his mind and shook him away from consciousness. He slept.

It might have been early morning when he had
made that strange visit to the camp of the Black
Hoods. By the measure of the sun across the floor
it was late afternoon when he lifted heavy
eyelids again. Takya gazed down upon him. Her
summons had brought him back just as her urging had sent him to sleep. He sat up with a smile,
but she did not return it.

"All is right?"

"We have time to make ready before we are put
to the test. Your mountain captain is not new to
this game. Matters of open warfare he under-
stands well, and he and his men have prepared a
rude welcome for those who come." Her faint
smile deepened. "I, too, have done my poor
best. Come and see."

He limped out on the terrace and for a moment
was startled. It was illusion, yes, but some of it
was real.

Jorik laughed at the expression on Craike's
face, inviting the Esper with a wave of the hand
to inspect the force he captained. There were
bowmen in plenty, standing sentinel on the
upper walls, arch, and tower, walking beats on
the twin buildings across the river. And it took
Craike a few seconds to sort out the ones he knew
from those who served Takya's purposes. But
the real had been so well posted as their illusory
companions. Nickus, for his superior accuracy
with the new weapon, held a vantage point on

the wall, and Zackuth was on the river arch where his arrows needed only a short range to be effective.

"Look below," Jorik urged, "and see what shall trip them up until we can pin them."

Again Craike blinked. The illusion was one he had seen before, but that had been a hurried erection on the part of a desperate girl; this was better contrived. All the ways leading to the river towers were cloaked with a tangled mass of thorn trees, the spiked branches interlocking into a wall no sword or spear could hope to pierce. It might be an illusion, but it would require a weighty counterspell on the part of the Hooded Ones to clear it.

"She takes some twigs Nickus finds, and a hair, and winds them together, then buried all under a stone. After she sings over it—and we have this!" Jorik babbled. "She is worth twenty hands—no, twice twenty hands, of fighting men, is the Lady Takya! Lord Ka-rak, I say that there is a new day coming for this land when such as you two stand up against the Hooded Ones."

"Aaaay." The warning was soft but clear, half whistle, half call. It issued from Nickus' lofty post. "They come!"

"So do they!" That was a sharp echo from Zackuth, "and down river as well."

"For which we have an answer." Jorik was undisturbed.

Those in the tower held their fire. To the confident attackers it was as such warfare had always been for them. If half their company was temporarily halted by the spiny maze, the river party had only to land on the offering rock and fight their way in, their efforts reinforced by the arts of their masters.

But, as their dugout nosed in, bow cords sang. There was a voiceless scream which tore through Craike's head as the hooded man in its bow clutched at the shaft protruding from his throat and fell forward into the river. Two more of the crew followed him, and the rest stopped paddling, dismayed. The current pulled them on under the arch, and Zackuth dropped a rock to good purpose. It carried one of the guardsmen down with it as it hit the craft squarely. The dugout turned over, spilling all the rest into the water.

Zackuth laughed; Jorik roared.

"Now they learn what manner of blood letting lies before them!" he cried so that his words must have reached the ears of the besiegers. "Let us see how eagerly they come to such feasting."

VIII

It was plain that the Black Hoods held their rulership by more practical virtues than courage. Having witnessed the smashing disaster of the river attack, they made no further move. Night was coming, and Craike watched them withdraw downstream with no elation. Nor did Jorik retain his cheerfulness.

"Now they will try something else. And since

we did not fall easily into their jaws, it will be harder to face. I do not like it that we must so face it during the hours of dark."

"There will be no dark," Takya countered. One slim finger pointed at a corner of the terrace, and up into the gathering dusk leaped a pencil of clear light. Slowly she turned and brought to life other torches on the roof of the tower over the river, on the arch spanning the water and on the parapet. In that radiance nothing could move unseen.

"So!" Her fingers snapped, and the beacons vanished. "When they are needed, we shall have them."

Jorik blinked. "Well enough, Lady. But honest fire is also good, and it provides warmth for a man's heart as well as light for his eyes."

She smiled as a mother might smile at a child. "Build your fire, Captain of Swords. But we shall have ample warning when the enemy comes." She called. A silent winged thing floated down and alighted on the arm she held out to invite it. The white owl, its eyes seeming to observe them all with intelligence, snapped its wicked beak as Takya stared back at it. Then with a flap of wings, it went.

"From us they may hide their thoughts and movements. But they can not close the sky to those things whose natural home it is. Be sure we shall know, and speedily, when they move against us."

They did not leave their posts however. Zackuth readied for action by laying up pieces of rubble which might serve as well as his first lucky shot.

It was a long night, wearing on the tempers o
all but Takya. Time and time again Craike triec
to probe the dark. But a blank wall was all he
met. Whatever moves the Black Hoods consid
ered, they were protected by an able barrier.

Jorik took to pacing back and forth on the
terrace, five strides one way, six the other, and he
brought down his bow with a little click on the
time-worn stones each time he turned.

"They are as busy hatching trouble as a fores
owl is in hatching an egg! But what kind o
trouble?"

Craike had schooled himself into an outwarc
patience. "For the learning of what we shall have
to wait. But why do they delay?"

Why did they? The more on edge he and hi
handful of defenders became, the easier mea
they were. He had no doubt that the Black Hood:
were fertile in surprise, though judging by wha
Takya and Jorik reported, they were not accus
tomed to such determined and resourcefu
opposition to their wills. Such opposition
would only firm their desire to wipe out the
rebels.

"They move." Takya's witch fires leaped from
every point she had earlier indicated. In tha
light she sped across the terrace to stand close te
Jorik and Craike and close to the parapet wall
"This is the lowest hour of the night, when the
blood runs slow and resistance is at its depth; so
they choose to move."

Jorik snapped his bow cord, and the thi
twang was a harp's note in the silence. But Takya
shook her head.

"Only the Hooded Ones come, and they are

well armored. See!" She jumped to the parapet and clapped her hands.

The witch light shown down on four standing within the thorn barrier, staring up from under the shadow of their hoods. An arrow sang, but it never reached its mark. Still feet away from the leader's breast, it fell to earth.

But Jorik refused to accept defeat. With all the force of his arm he sent a second shaft after the first. It, too, landed at the feet of the silent four. Craike grasped at Takya, but she eluded him, moving to call down to the Hooded Ones.

"What would you, Men of Power, a truce?"

"Daughter of evil, you are not alone. Let us speak with your lord."

She laughed, shaking out her unbound hair, rippling it through her fingers, gloatingly. "Does this show that I have taken a lord, Men of Power? Takya is herself, without division still. Let that hope die from your hearts. I ask you again, what is it you wish, a truce?"

"Set forth your lord; with him we will bargain."

She smoothed back her hair impatiently. "I have no lord; I and my power are intact. Try me and see, Tousuth. Yes, I know you Tousuth, the Master, and Salsbal, Bulan, Yily." She told them off with a pointed forefinger, like a child counting in some game.

Jorik stirred and drew in a sharp breath, and the men below shifted position. Craike caught thoughts. To use a man's name in the presence of hostile powers was magic indeed.

"Takya!" It was a reptile's hiss.

Again she laughed. "Ah, but the first naming was mine, Tousuth. Did you believe me so poor and power lost that I would obey you tamely? I did not at the horning; why should I now when I stand free of you? Before you had to use Takyi to capture me. But Takyi is gone into the far darkness, and over me now you can lay no such net! Also, I have summoned one beside me—" Her hand closed on Craike's arm, drawing him forward.

He faced the impact of those eyes meeting them squarely. Raising his hand he told them off as the girl had done:

"Tousuth, Master of women baiters, Salsbal, Bulan, Yily, the wolves who slink behind him. I am here, what would you have of me?"

But they were silent, and he could feel them searching him out, making thrusts against his mind shield, learning in their turn that he was of their kind; he was Esper born.

"What would you have?" he repeated more loudly. "If you do not wish to treat, then leave the night undisturbed for honest men's sleep."

"Changeling!" It was Tousuth who spat that. It was his turn to point a finger and chant a sentence or two, his men watching him with confidence.

But Craike, remembering that other scene before Sampur, was trying a wild experiment of his own. He concentrated upon the man Takya had named Yily, his black cloak and black hood making a vulture's shadow against the rock. Vulture—vulture!

He did not know that he had pointed to his chosen victim, nor that he was repeating that word aloud in the same intonation as Tousuth's chant. "Vulture!"

A cool hand closed about his other wrist, and from that contact power flowed to join his. It was pointed, launched.

"Vulture!"

A black bird flapped and screamed, arose on beating wings to fly at him, raw, red head outstretched, beak agap. Then a scream of agony and despair and a black cloaked man writhed out his life on the slope by the thorn thicket.

"Good!" Takya cried. "That was well done, Ka-rak, very well done! But you can not use that weapon a second time."

Craike was filled with a wild elation, and he did not listen to her. His finger already indicated Bulan and he was chanting: "Dog—"

But to no purpose. The Black Hood did not drop to all fours, he remained human; and Craike's voice faded. Takya spoke in a swift whisper:

"They are warned; you can never march against them twice by the same path. Only because they were unprepared did you succeed. Ho, Tousuth," she called, "do you now believe that we are well armed? Speak with a true tongue and say what you want of us."

"Yes," Jorik boomed, "you can not take us, Master of Power. Go your way, and we shall go ours."

"There can not be two powers in any land, as you should know, Jorik of the Eagles' Tower,

who tried once before to prove that and suffered
thereby. There must be a victor here, and to the
vanquished—naught!"

Craike could see the logic in that. But the master was continuing: "As to what we want here; it
is a decision. Match your power against ours,
changeling. And since you have not taken the
witch, use her also if you wish. In the end it will
come to the same thing, for both of you must be
rendered helpless."

"Here and now?" asked Craike.

"Dawn comes; it will soon be another day. By
sun or shadow, we care not in such a battle."

The elation of his quick success in that first try
was gone. Craike fingered the bow he had not yet
used. He shrank inwardly from the contest the
other proposed; he was too uncertain of his powers. One victory had come from too little knowledge. Takya's hand curled about his stiff fingers
once again. The impish mockery was back in her
voice, ruffling his temper, irritating him into
defiance.

"Show them what you can do, Lord Ka-rak,
you who can master illusions."

He glanced down at her, and the sight of that
cropped lock of hair at her temple gave him an
odd confidence. Neither was Takya as all-
powerful as she would have him believe.

"I accept your challenge," he called. "Let it be
here and now."

"We accept your challenge!" Takya's flash of
annoyance, her quick correction, pleased him.
Before the echo of her words died away she
hurled her first attack.

Witch fire leaped down slope to ring in the three men, playing briefly along the body of the dead Yily. It flickered up and down about their feet and legs so they stood washed in pallid flame. While about their heads darted winged shapes which might have been owls or other night hunters.

There was a malignant hissing, and the slope sprouted reptiles, moving in a wave. Illusions? All, or some, designed, Craike understood, to divert the enemy's minds. He added a few of his own: a wolfish shape crouching in the shadow, leaping, to vanish as its paws cut the witch fire.

Swift as had been Takya's attack, so did those below parry. An oppressive weight, so tangible that Craike looked up to see if some mountain threatened them from overhead, began to close down upon the parapet. He heard a cry of alarm. There *was* a black cloud to be seen now, a giant press closing upon them.

Balls of witch fire flashed out of the light pillars and darted at those on the parapet. One flew straight at Craike's face, its burning breath singeing his skin.

"Fool!" Takya's thought was a whip lash. "Illusions are only real for the believer."

He steadied, and the witch ball vanished. But he was badly shaken. This was outside any Esper training he had had; it was the very thing he had been conditioned against. He felt slow, clumsy, and he was ashamed that upon Takya must the burden of their defense now rest.

Upon her—Craike's eyes narrowed. He loosened her hold on him and did not try to contact her. There was too much chance of self-betrayal in that. His plan was utterly wild, but it had been well demonstrated that the Black Hoods could only be caught by the unexpected.

Another witch ball hurtled at him, and he leaped to the terrace, landing with a force which sent a lance of pain up his healing leg. But on the parapet a Craike still stood, shoulder to shoulder with Takya. To maintain that illusion was a task which made him sweat as he crept silently away from the tower.

He had made a security guard to astonish Takya, the wolf, all the other illusions. But they had been only wisps, things alive for the moment with no need for elaboration. To hold this semblance of himself was in some ways easier, some ways harder. It was easier to make, for the image was produced of self-knowledge, and it was harder, for it was meant to deceive masters of illusion.

Craike reached the steps to the rock of the offerings. The glow of the witch lights here was pale, and the ledge below dark. He crept down, one arrow held firmly in his hand.

Here the sense of oppression was a hundred-fold worse, and he moved as one wading through a flood which entrapped limbs and brain. Blind, he went to all fours, feeling his way to the river.

He set the arrow between his teeth in a bite which indented its shaft. A knife would have been far better, but he had no time to beg Jorik's. He slipped over, shivering as the chill water took him. Then he swam under the arch.

It was comparatively easy to reach the shingle

where the dugout of the Black Hoods had turned over. As he made his way to the shore he brushed against water-soaked cloth and realized he shared this scrap of gravel with the dead. Then, the arrow still between his teeth, Craike climbed up behind the Black Hoods' position.

IX

The thorn hedge cloaked the rise above him. But he concentrated on the breaking of that illusion, wading on through a mass of thorns, intact to his eyes, thin air at his passing. Then he was behind the Black Hoods. Takya stood, a black and white figure on the wall above, beside the illusion Craike.

Now!

The illusion Craike swelled a little more than life size, while his creator gathered his feet under him, preparatory to attack. The Craike on the wall altered—anything to hold the attention of Tousuth for a crucial second or two. A monster grew from the man: wings, horns, curved tusks, all the embellishments Craike's imagination could add. He heard shouts from the tower.

But with the arrow as a dagger in his hand, he sprang, allowing himself in that moment to see only, to think only of a point on Tousuth's back.

The head drove in and in, and Tousuth went down on his knees, clutching at his chest, coughing; while Craike, with a savagery he had not known he possessed, leaned on the shaft to drive it deeper.

Fingers hooked about Craike's throat, cutting off air, dragging him back. He was pulled from Tousuth, loosing his hold on the arrow shaft to tear at the hands denying him breath. There was a red fog which even the witch lights could not pierce, and the roaring in his head was far louder than the shouts from the tower.

Then he was flat on the ground, still moving feebly. But the hands were gone from his throat, and he gasped in air. Around him circled balls of fire, dripping, twirling, he closed his eyes against their glare.

"Lord—Lord!"

The hail reached him only faintly. Hands pulled at him, and he tried to resist. But when he opened his eyes it was to see Jorik's brown face. Jorik was at the tower. How had Craike returned there? Surely he *had* attacked Tousuth? Or was it an illusion?

"He is not dead."

Whether or not that was said to him, Craike did not know; but his fingers were at his throat, and he winced from his own touch. Then an arm came under his shoulders, lifting him, and he had a dizzy moment until earth and gray sky settled into their proper places.

Takya was there, with Nickus and Zackuth hovering in the background of black jerkined guardsmen who stared back at her sullenly over the bodies of the dead. For they were all dead— the Hooded Ones. There was Tousuth, his head in the sand. His fellows were crumpled beside him.

The witch girl chanted, and in her hands was a

cat's cradle of black strands. The men who followed Tousuth cringed, and their fear was a
cloud Craike could see. He grabbed at Jorik, won
to his feet, and tried to hail Takya. But not even a
croak came from his tortured throat. So he flung
himself at her, one hand out like a sword blade to
slash. It fell across that wicked net of hair, breaking it, and went to close upon Takya's wrist in a
crushing grip.

"Enough!" He could get out that command
mind to mind.

She drew in upon herself as a cat crouches for
a spring, and spat, her eyes green with feral
lusting fire. But he had an answer to that, read it
in her own spark of fear at his touch. His hands
twined in her hair.

"They are men." He pulled those black strands
to emphasize his words. "They only obeyed orders. We have a quarrel with their masters, but
not with them!"

"They hunted, and now they shall be hunted!"

"I have been hunted, as have you, witch woman. While I live there shall be no more such
hunts, whether I am hound or quarry."

"While you live—" Her menace was ready.

Suddenly Craike forced out a hoarse croak
meant for laughter. "You, yourself, Takya, have
put the arrow to this bow cord!"

He kept one hand tangled in her hair. But with
the other he snatched from her belt the knife she
had borrowed from Nickus and not returned.
She screamed, beat against him with her fists
and tried to bite. He mastered her roughly, not

loosing his grip on that black silk. And then in sweeps of that well whetted blade he did what the Black Hoods had failed in doing, he sawed through those lengths.

"I am leaving you no weapons, Takya. You shall not rule here as you have thought to do." The exultation he had known when he had won his first victory against the Black Hoods was returning a hundredfold. "For a while I shall pull those pretty claws of yours!" He wondered briefly how long it would take her hair to regrow. At least they would have a breathing spell before her powers returned.

Then, his arm still prisoning her shoulders, the mass of her hair streaming free from his left hand, he turned to face the guardsmen.

"Tell them to go," he thought, "taking their dead with them."

"You will go, taking these with you," she repeated aloud, stony and calm.

One of the men dropped to his knees by Tousuth's body, then abased himself before Craike.

"We are your hounds, Master."

Craike found his voice at last. "You are no man's hounds, for you are a man. Get you gone to Sampur and tell them that the power is no longer to make hind nor hound. If there are those who wish to share the fate of Tousuth, perhaps when they look upon him as dead they will think more of it."

"Lord, do you come also to Sampur to rule?" the other asked timidly.

Craike laughed. "Not until I have established

my lordship elsewhere. Get you back to Sampur
and trouble us no more."

He turned his back on the guardsmen and,
drawing the silent Takya, still within the circle
of his arm, he started back to the tower. The
bowmen remained behind, and Craike and the
girl were alone as they reached the upper level.
He paused then and looked down into her set,
expressionless face.

"What shall I do with you?"

"You have shamed me and taken my power
from me. What does a warrior do with a female
slave?" She formed a stark mind picture, hurling
it at him as she had hurled the stone on the mesa.

With his left hand he whipped her hair across
her face, smarting under that taunt.

"I have taken no slave, nor any woman in that
fashion, nor shall I. Go your way, Takya, and
fight me again if you wish when your hair has
grown."

She studied him, and her astonishment was
plain. Then she laughed and clutched at the hair,
tearing it free from his grasp, bundling it into the
front of her single garment.

"So be it, Ka-rak. It is war between us. But I am
not departing hence yet a while." She broke
away, and he could hear the scuff of her feet on
the steps as she climbed to her own chamber in
the tower.

"They are on their way, Lord, and they will
keep to it." Jorik came up. He stretched. "It was a
battle not altogether to my liking. For the honest
giving of blows from one's hand is better than all
this magic, potent as it is."

Craike sat down beside the fire. He could not have agreed more heartily with any suggestion. Now that it was over he felt drained of energy.

"I do not believe they will return," he wheezed hoarsely, very conscious of his bruised throat.

Nickus chuckled, and Zackuth barked his own laughter.

"Seeing how you handled the Lady, Lord, they want nothing more than to be out of your grasp and that as speedily as possible. Nor, when those of Sampur see what they bring with them, do I think we shall be sought out by others bearing drawn swords. Now," Jorik slapped his fat middle, "I could do with meat in my belly. And you, Lord, have taken such handling as needs good food to counter."

There was no mention of Takya, nor did any go to summon her when the meat was roasted. And Craike was content to have it so. He was too tired for any more heroics.

Nickus hummed a soft tune as he rubbed down his unstrung bow before wrapping it away from the river damp. And Craike was aware that the younger man glanced at him slyly when he thought the Esper's attention elsewhere. Jorik, too, appeared highly amused at some private thoughts, and he had fallen to beating time with one finger to Nickus' tune. Craike shifted uncomfortably. He was an actor who had forgotten his lines, a novice required to make a ritual move he did not understand. What they wanted of him he could not guess, for he was too tired to mind touch. He only wanted sleep, and that he sought as soon as he painfully swallowed his last bite.

But he heard through semistupor, a surprised exclamation from Nickus.

"He goes not to seek her—to take her!"

Jorik's answer held something of approval in it. "To master such as the Lady Takya he will need full strength of power and limb. His is the wisest way, not to gulp the fruits of battle before the dust of the last charge is laid. She is his by shearing, but she is no meek ewe to come readily under any man's hand."

Takya did not appear the next day, nor the next. And Craike made no move to climb to her. His companions elaborately did not notice her absence as they worked together, setting in place fallen stones, bringing the tower into a better state of repair, or killing deer to smoke the meat. For as Jorik pointed out:

"Soon comes the season of cold. We must build us a snug place and have food under our hands before then." He broke off and gazed thoughtfully down stream. "This is also the fair time when countrymen bring their wares to market. There are traders in Sampur. We could offer our hides, even though they be newly fleshed, for salt and grain. And a bow—this Kaluf of whom you have spoken, would he not give a good price for a bow?"

Craike raised an eyebrow. "Sampur? But they have little cause to welcome us in Sampur."

"You and the Lady Takya, Lord, they might take arms against in fear. But if Zackuth and I went in the guise of wandering hunters—and Zackuth is of the Children of Noe, he could trade privately with his kin. We must have supplies,

Lord, before the coming of the cold, and this is too fine a fortress to abandon."

So it was decided that Jorik and Zackuth were to try their luck with the traders. Nickus went to hunt, wrecking havoc among the flocks of migrating fowl, and Craike held the tower alone.

As he turned from seeing them away, he sighted the owl wheel out from the window slit of the upper chamber, its mournful cry sounding loud. On sudden impulse he went inside to climb the stair. There had been enough of her sulking. He sent that thought before him as an order. She did not reply. Craike's heart beat faster. Was—had she gone? The rough outer wall, was it possible to climb down that?

He flung himself up the last few steps and burst into the room. She was standing there, her shorn head high as if she and not he had been the victor. When he saw her Craike stopped. Then he moved again, faster than he had climbed those stairs. For in that moment the customs of this world were clear, he knew what he must do, what he wanted to do. If this revelation was some spell of Takya's he did not care.

Later he was aroused by the caress of silk on his body, felt her cool fingers as he had felt them drawing the poison from his wounds. It was a black belt, and she was making fast about him, murmuring words softly as she interwove strand with strand about his waist until there was no beginning nor end to be detected.

"My chain on you, man of power." Her eyes slanted down at him.

He buried both his hands in the ragged crop of hair from which those threads had been severed and so held her quiet for his kiss.

"My seal upon you, witch."

"What Tousuth would have done, you have accomplished for him," she observed pensively when he had given her a measure of freedom once again. "Only through you may I now use my power."

"Which is perhaps well for this land and those who dwell in it," he laughed. "We are now tied to a common destiny, my lady of river towers."

She sat up running her hands through her hair with some of her old caress.

"It will grow again," he consoled.

"To no purpose, except to pleasure my vanity. Yes, we are tied together. But you do not regret it, Ka-rak—"

"Neither do you, witch." There was no longer any barrier between their minds, as there was none between their bodies. "What destiny will you now spin for the two of us?"

"A great one. Tousuth knew my power-to-come. I would now realize it." Her chin went up. "And you with me, Ka-rak. By this," her hand rested lightly on the belt.

"Doubtless you will set us up as rulers over Sampur?" he said lazily.

"Sampur!" she sniffed. "This world is wide— Her arms went out as if to encircle all which lay beyond the tower walls.

Craike drew her back to him jealously. "For that there is more than time enough. This is an hour for something else, even in a warlock's world."

THROUGH THE NEEDLE'S EYE

IT WAS NOT her strange reputation which attracted me to old Miss Ruthevan, though there were stories to excite a solitary child's morbid taste. Rather it was what she was able to create, opening a whole new world to the crippled girl I was thirty years ago.

Two years before I made that momentous visit to Cousin Althea I suffered an attack of what was then known as infantile paralysis. In those days before Salk, there was no cure. I was fourteen when I met Miss Ruthevan, and I had been told for weary months that I was lucky to be able to walk at all, even though I must do so with a heavy brace on my right leg. I might accept that verdict outwardly, but the me imprisoned in the thin adolescent's body was a rebel.

Cousin Althea's house was small, and on the wrong side of the wrong street to claim gentility. (Cramwell did not have a railroad to separate the comfortable, smug sheep from the aspiring goats.) But her straggling back garden ran to a wall of mellow, red brick patterned by green moss, and in one place a section of this barrier had broken down so one could hitch up to look into the tangled mat of vine and brier which now covered most of the Ruthevan domain.

Three-fourths of that garden had reverted to the wild, but around the bulk of the house it was kept in some order. The fat, totally deaf old woman who ruled Miss Ruthevan's domestic concerns could often be seen poking about, snipping off flowers or leaves, after examining each with the care of a cautious shopper or filling a pan with wizened berries. Birds loved the Ruthevan garden and built whole colonies of nests in its unpruned trees. Bees and butterflies were thick in the undisturbed peace. Though I longed to explore, I never quite dared, until the day of the quilt.

That had been a day of disappointment. There was a Sunday school picnic to which Ruth, Cousin Althea's daughter, and I were invited. I knew that it was not for one unable to play ball, race or swim. Proudly I refused to go, giving the mendacious excuse that my leg ached. Filled with bitter envy, I watched Ruth leave. I refused Cousin Althea's offer to let me make candy, marching off, lurch-push to perch on the wall.

There was something new in the garden beyond. An expanse of color flapped languidly from a clothes line, giving tantalizing glimpses of it. Before I knew it, I tumbled over the wall, acquiring a goodly number of scrapes and bruises on the way, and struggled through a straggle of briers to see better.

It was worth my struggle. Cousin Althea had quilts in plenty, mostly made by Grandma Moss, who was considered by the family to be an artist at needlework. But what I viewed now was as clearly above the best efforts of Grandma as a Rembrandt above an inn sign.

This was appliqué work, each block of a different pattern; though, after some study, I became aware that the whole was to be a panorama of autumn. There were flowers, fruits, berries and nuts, each with their attendant clusters of leaves, while the border was an interwoven wreath of maple and oak foliage in the richest coloring. Not only was the appliqué so perfect one could not detect a single stitch, but the quilting overpattern was as delicate as lace. It was old; its once white background had been time-dyed cream; and it was the most beautiful thing I had ever seen.

"Well, what do you think of it?"

I lurched as I tried to turn quickly, catching for support at the trunk of a gnarled apple tree. On the brick walk from the house stood old Miss Ruthevan. She was tall and held herself stiffly straight, the masses of her thick, white hair built into a formal coil which, by rights, should have supported a tiara. From throat to instep she was covered by a loose robe in a neutral shade of blue-gray which fully concealed her body.

Ruth had reported Miss Ruthevan to be a terrifying person; her nickname among the children was "old witch." But after my first flash

of panic, I was not alarmed, being too bemused
by the quilt.

"I think it's wonderful. All fall things—"

"It's a bride quilt," she replied shortly, "made
for a September bride."

She moved and lost all her majesty of person,
for she limped in an even more ungainly fashion
than I, weaving from side to side as if about to
lose her balance at any moment. When she
halted and put her hand on the quilt, she was
once more an uncrowned queen. Her face was
paper white, her lips blue lines. But her sunken,
very alive eyes probed me.

"Who are you?"

"Ernestine Williams. I'm staying with Cousin
Althea." I pointed to the wall.

Her thin brows, as white as her hair, drew into
a small frown. Then she nodded. "Catherine
Moss's granddaughter, yes. Do you sew, Ernestine?"

I shook my head, oddly ashamed. There was a
vast importance to that question, I felt. Maybe
that gave me the courage to add, "I wish I
could—like that." I pointed a finger at the quilt.
I surprised myself, for never before had I
wished to use a needle.

Miss Ruthevan's clawlike hand fell heavily on
my shoulder. She swung her body around awk-
wardly, using me as a pivot, and then drew me
along with her. I strove to match my limp to her
wider lurch, up three worn steps into a hallway,
which was very dark and cool out of the sun.

Shut doors flanked us, but the one at the far
end stood open, and there she brought me, still

captive in her strong grasp. Once we were inside she released me, to make her own crab's way to a tall-backed chair standing in the full light of a side window. There she sat enthroned, as was right and proper.

An embroidery frame stood before the chair, covered with a throw of white cloth. At her right hand was a low table bearing a rack of innumerable, small spindles, each wound with colorful thread.

"Look around," she commanded. "You are a Moss. Catherine Moss had some skill; maybe you have inherited it."

I was ready to disclaim any of my grandmother's talent; but Miss Ruthevan, drawing off the shield cloth and folding it with small flicks, ignored me. So I began to edge nervously about the room, staring wide-eyed at the display there.

The walls were covered with framed, glass-protected needlework. Those pieces to my left were very old, the colors long faded, the exquisite stitchery almost too dim to see. But, as I made my slow progress, each succeeding picture became brighter and more distinct. Some were the conventional samplers, but the majority were portraits or true pictures. As I skirted needlework chairs and dodged a fire screen, I saw that the art was in use everywhere. I was in a shrine to needle creations which had been brought to the highest peak of perfection and beauty. As I made that journey of discovery, Miss Ruthevan stitched away the minutes, pausing now and then to study a single half-open white rose in a small vase on her table.

"Did you make all these, Miss Ruthevan?" I
blurted out at last.

She took two careful stitches before she
answered. "No. There have always been Ruthevan women so talented, for three hundred
years. It began"—her blue lips curved in a very
small shadow of a smile, though she did not
turn her attention from her work—"with Grizel
Ruthevan, of a family a king chose to
outlaw—which was, perhaps, hardly wise of
him." She raised her hand and pointed with the
needle she held to the first of the old frames. It
seemed to me that a sparkle of sunlight gathered on the needle and lanced through the
shadows about the picture she so indicated.
"Grizel Ruthevan, aged seventeen—she was the
first of us. But there were enough to follow. I am
the last."

"You mean your—your ancestors—did all
this."

Again she smiled that curious smile. "Not all
of them, my dear. Our art requires a certain cast
of mind, a talent you may certainly call it. My
own aunt, for example did not have it; and, of
course, my mother, not being born a Ruthevan,
did not. But my great-aunt Vannessa was very
able."

I do not know how it came about, but when I
left, I was committed to the study of needlework
under Miss Ruthevan's teaching; though she
gave me to understand from the first that the
perfection I saw about me was not the result of
amateur work, and that here, as in all other arts,
patience and practice as well as aptitude were
needed.

I went home full of the wonders of what I had seen; and when I cut single-mindedly across Ruth's account of her day, she roused to counterattack.

"She's a witch, you know!" She teetered back and forth on the boards of the small front porch. "She makes people disappear; maybe she'll do that to you if you hang around over there."

"Ruthie!" Cousin Althea, her face flushed from baking, stood behind the patched screen. Her daughter was apprehensively quiet as she came out. But I was more interested in what Ruthie had said than any impending scolding.

"Makes people disappear—how?"

"That's an untruth, Ruthie," my cousin said firmly. True to her upbringing, Cousin Althea thought the word "lie" coarse. "Never let me hear you say a thing like that about Miss Ruthevan again. She has had a very sad life—"

"Because she's lame?" I challenged.

Cousin Althea hesitated; truth won over tact. "Partly. You'd never think it to look at her now, but when she was just a little older than you girls she was a real beauty. Why, I remember mother telling about how people would go to their windows just to watch her drive by with her father, the Colonel. He had a team of matched grays and a carriage he'd bought in New York.

"She went away to school, too, Anne Ruthevan did. And that's where she met her sweetheart. He was the older brother of one of her schoolmates."

"But Miss Ruthevan's an old maid!" Ruth protested. "She didn't ever marry."

"No." Cousin Althea sat down in the old, wooden porch rocker and picked up a palm leaf fan to cool her face, "No, she didn't ever marry. All her good fortune turned bad almost overnight, you might say.

"She and her father went out driving. It was late August and she was planning to be married in September. There was a bad storm came up very sudden. It frightened those grays and they ran away down on the river road. They didn't make the turn there and the carriage was smashed up. The Colonel was killed. Miss Anne—well, for days everybody thought she'd die, too.

"Her sweetheart came up from New York. My mother said he was the handsomest man: tall, with black hair waving down a little over his forehead. He stayed with the Chambers family. Mr. Chambers was Miss Anne's uncle on her mother's side. He tried every day to see Miss Anne, only she would never have him in—she must have known by then—"

"That she was always going to be lame," I said flatly.

Cousin Althea did not look at me when she nodded agreement.

"He went away, finally. But he kept coming back. After a while people guessed what was really going on. It wasn't Miss Anne he was coming to see now; it was her cousin, Rita Chambers.

"By then Miss Anne had found out some other pretty unhappy things. The Colonel had died sudden, and he left his business in a big tangle.

By the time someone who knew how got to looking after it most of the money was gone. Here was Miss Anne, brought up to have most of what she had a mind for; and now she had nothing. Losing her sweetheart to Rita and then her money; it changed her. She shut herself away from most folks. She was awful young—only twenty.

"Pretty soon Rita was planning her wedding—they were going to be married in August, just about a year after that ride which changed Miss Anne's life. Her fiancé came up from New York a couple of days ahead of time; he was staying at Doc Bernard's. Well, the wedding day came, and Doc was to drive the groom to the church. He waited a good long time and finally went up to his room to hurry him along a little, but he wasn't there. His clothes were all laid out, nice and neat. I remember hearing Mrs. Bernard, she was awfully old then, telling as how it gave her a turn to see the white rose he was to wear in his buttonhole still sitting in a glass of water on the chest of drawers. But he was gone—didn't take his clothes nor nothing—just went. Nobody saw hide nor hair of him afterwards."

"But what could have happened to him, Cousin Althea?" I asked.

"They did some hunting around, but never found anyone who saw him after breakfast that morning. Most people finally decided he was ashamed of it all, that he felt it about Miss Anne. 'Course, that didn't explain why he left his clothes all lying there. Mother always said she thought both Anne and Rita were well rid of him.

It was a ten day's wonder all right, but people forgot in time. The Chamberses took Rita away to a watering place for a while; she was pretty peeked. Two years later she married John Ford; he'd always been sweet on her. Then they moved out west someplace. I heard as how she'd taken a dislike to this whole town and told John she'd say 'yes' to him provided he moved.

"Since then—well, Miss Anne, she began to do a little better. She was able to get out of bed that winter and took to sewing—not making clothes and such, but embroidery. Real important people have bought some of her fancy pictures; I heard tell a couple are even in museums. And you're a very lucky girl, Ernestine, if she'll teach you like you said."

It was not until I was in bed that night, going over my meeting with Miss Ruthevan and Cousin Althea's story, that something gave me a queer start: the thought of that unclaimed white rose.

Most of the time I had spent with Miss Ruthevan she had been at work. But I had never seen the picture she was stitching, only her hands holding the needle dipping in and out, or bringing a thread into the best light as she matched it against the petals of the rose on her table.

That had been a perfect rose; it might have been carved from ivory. Miss Ruthevan had not taken it out of the glass; she had not moved out of her chair when I left. But now I was sure that, when I had looked back from the door, the rose had been gone. Where? It was a puzzle. But, of course, Miss Ruthevan must have done some-

thing with it when I went to look at some one of
the pictures she had called to my attention.

Cousin Althea was flattered that Miss Ruthevan had shown interest in me; I know my retell-
ing of the comment about Grandma Moss had
pleased her greatly. She carefully supervised my
dress before my departure for the Ruthevan
house the next day, and she would not let me
take the shortcut through the garden. I must limp
around the block and approach properly
through the front door. I did, uncomfortable in
the fresh folds of skirt, so ill looking I believed,
above the ugliness of the brace.

Today Miss Ruthevan had put aside the covered frame and was busied instead with a delicate length of old lace, matching thread with
extra care. It was a repair job for a museum, she
told me.

She put me to work helping her with the
thread. Texture, color, shading—I must have an
eye for all, she told me crisply. She spun some of
her thread herself and dyed much of it, using
formulas which the Ruthevan women had de-
veloped over the years.

So through the days and weeks which followed I found cool refuge in that high-walled
room where I was allowed to handle precious
fabrics and take some part in her work. I learned
to spin on a wheel older than much of the town,
and I worked in the small shed-like summer
kitchen skimming dye pots and watching Miss
Ruthevan measure bark and dried leaves and
roots in careful quantities.

It was only rarely that she worked on the piece

in the standing frame, which she never allowed me to see. She did not forbid that in words, merely arranged it so that I did not. But from time to time, when she had a perfectly formed fern, a flower, and once in the early morning when a dew-beaded spider web cornered the window without, she would stitch away. I never saw what she did with her models when she had finished. I only knew that when the last stitch was set to her liking, the vase was empty, the web had vanished.

She had a special needle for this work. It was kept in a small brass box, and she made a kind of ceremony of opening the box, holding it tightly to her breast, with her eyes closed; she also took a great while to thread the needle itself, running the thread back and forth through it. But when Miss Ruthevan did not choose to explain, there was that about her which kept one from asking questions.

I learned, slowly and painfully, with pricked fingers and sick frustration each time I saw how far below my goals my finished work was. But there was a great teacher in Miss Ruthevan. She had patience and her criticism inspired instead of blighted. Once I brought her a shell I had found. She turned it over, putting it on her model table. When I came the next day it still lay there, but on a square of fabric, the outline of the shell sketched upon the cloth.

"Select your threads," she told me.

It took me a long time to match and rematch. She examined my choice and made no changes.

"You have the eye. If you can also learn the skill . . ."

I tried to reproduce the shell; but the painful difference between my work and the model exasperated me, until the thread knotted and snarled and I was close to tears. She took it out of my hand.

"You try too hard. You think of the stitches instead of the whole. It must be done here as well as with your fingers." She touched one of her cool, dry fingers to my forehead.

So I learned patience as well as skill, and as she worked Miss Ruthevan spoke of art and artists, of the days when she had gone out of Cramwell into a world long lost. I went back to Cousin Althea's each afternoon with my head full of far places and the beauty men and women would create. Sometimes she had me leaf through books of prints, or spend afternoons sorting out patterns inscribed on strips of parchment older than my own country.

The change in Miss Ruthevan herself came so slowly during those weeks that I did not note it at first. When she began to refuse commissions, I was not troubled, but rather pleased, for she spent more time with me, only busy with that on the standing frame. I did regret her refusing to embroider a wedding dress; it was so beautiful. It was that denial which made me aware that now she seldom came out of her chair; there were no more mornings with the dye pots.

One day when I came there were no sounds from the kitchen, a curious silence in the house.

My uneasiness grew as I entered the workroom to see Miss Ruthevan sitting with folded hands, no needle at work. She turned her head to watch as I limped across the carpet. I spoke the first thing in my mind.

"Miss Applebee's gone." I had never seen much of the deaf housekeeper, but the muted sounds of her presence had always been with us. I missed them now.

"Yes, Lucy is gone. Our time has almost run out. Sit down, Ernestine. No, do not reach for your work, I have something to say to you."

That sounded a little like a scolding to come. I searched my conscience as she continued.

"Some day very soon now, Ernestine, I too, shall go."

I stared at her, frightened. For the first time I was aware of just how old Miss Ruthevan must be, how skeleton thin were her quiet hands.

She laughed. "Don't grow so big-eyed, child. I have no intention of being coffined, none at all. It is just that I have earned a vacation of sorts, one of my own choosing. Remember this, Ernestine, nothing in this world comes to us unpaid for; and when I speak of pay, I do not talk of money. Things which may be bought with money are the easy things. No, the great desires of our hearts are paid for in other coin; I have paid for what I want most, with fifty years of labor. Now the end is in sight—see for yourself!"

She pushed at the frame so for the first time I could see what it held.

It was a picture, a vivid one. Somehow I felt that I looked through a window to see reality. In the background to the left, tall trees arched, wearing the brilliant livery of fall. In the foreground was a riot of flowers.

Against a flaming oak stood a man, a shaft of light illuminating his high-held, dark head. His thin face was keenly alive and welcoming. His hair waved down a little over his forehead.

Surrounded by the flowers was the figure of a woman. By the grace and slenderness of her body she was young. But her face was still but blank canvas.

I went closer, fascinated by form and color, seeing more details the longer I studied it. There was a rabbit crouched beneath a clump of fern, and at the feet of the girl a cat, eyeing the hunter with the enigmatic scrutiny of its kind. Its striped, gray and black coat was so real I longed to touch—to see if it were truly fur.

"That was Timothy," Miss Ruthevan said suddenly. "I did quite well with him. He was so old, so old and tired. Now he will be forever young."

"But you haven't done the lady's face." I ventured.

"Not yet, child, but soon now." She suddenly tossed the cover over the frame to hide it all.

"There is this." She picked up the brass needle-case and opened it fully for the first time, to display a strip of threadbare velvet into which was thrust two needles. They were not the ordinary steel ones, such as I had learned to use, but bright yellow slivers of fire in the sun.

"Once," she told me, "there were six of these—now only two. This one is mine. And

this," her finger did not quite touch the last,
"shall be yours, if you wish, only if you wish,
Ernestine. Always remember one pays a price for
power. If tomorrow, or the day after, you come
and find me gone, you shall also find this box
waiting for you. Take it and use the needle if and
when you will—but carefully. Grizel Ruthevan
bought this box for a very high price indeed. I do
not know whether we should bless or curse her.
. . ." Her voice trailed away and I knew without
any formal dismissal I was to go. But at the door I
hesitated to look back.

Miss Ruthevan had pulled the frame back into
working distance before her. As I watched she
made a careful selection of thread, set it in the
needle's waiting eye. She took one stitch and
then another. I went into the dark silence of the
hall. Miss Ruthevan was finishing the picture.

I said nothing to Cousin Althea of that curious
interview. The next day I went almost secretly
into the Ruthevan house by the way I had first
entered it, over the garden wall. The silence was
even deeper than it had been the afternoon before. There was a curious deadness to it, like the
silence of a house left unoccupied. I crept to the
workroom; there was no one in the chair by the
window. I had not really expected to find her
there.

When I reached the chair, something seemed
to sap my strength so I sat in it as all those days I
had seen her sit. The picture stood in its frame
facing me—uncovered. As I had expected, it was
complete. The imperiously beautiful face of the
lady was there in detail. I recognized those wing

brows, though now they were dark, the eyes, the mouth with its shadow smile; recognized them with a shiver. Now I knew where the rose, the fern, the web and all the other models had gone. I also knew, without being told, the meaning of the gold needles and why the maiden in the picture wore Anne Ruthevan's face and the hunter had black hair.

I ran, and I was climbing over the back wall before I was truly aware of what I did. But weighing down the pocket of my sewing apron was the brass needle-box. I have never opened it. I am not Miss Ruthevan; I have not the determination, nor perhaps the courage, to pay the price such skill demands. With whom—or *what*—Grizel Ruthevan dealt to acquire those needles, I do not like to think at all.

BY A HAIR

You SAY, FRIEND, that witchcraft at its strongest is but a crude knowledge of psychology, a use of a man's own fear of the unknown to destroy him? Perhaps it may be so in modern lands. But me, I have seen what I have seen. More than fear destroyed Dagmar Kark and Colonel Andrei Veroff.

There were four of them, strong and passionate: Ivor and Dagmar Kark, Andrei Varoff and the Countess Ana. What they desired they gained by the aid of something not to be seen nor felt nor sensed tangibly, something not in the experience of modern man.

Ivor was an idealist who held to a cause and the woman he thought Dagmar to be. Dagmar, she wanted power—power over the kind of man who could give her all her heart desired. And so she wanted Colonel Andrei Varoff.

And Varoff, his wish was a common one,

though odd for one of his creed. When a man has been nourished on the belief that the state is all, the individual nothing, it is queer to want a son to the point of obsession. And, though Varoff had taken many women, none had produced a child he could be sure was his.

The Countess Ana, she wanted justice—and love.

The four people had faith in themselves, strong faith. Besides, they had it in other things—Ivor in his cause and his wife, Varoff in a creed. And Dagmar and Ana in something very old and enduring.

It could not have happened in this new land of yours, to that I agree; but in my birth country it is different. All this came to be in a narrow knife slash of a valley running from mountains to the gray salt sweep of the Baltic. It is true that the shadow of the true cross has lain over that valley since the Teutonic knights planted it on the castle they built in the crags almost a thousand years ago. But before the white Christ came, other, grimmer gods were worshiped in that land. In the fir forest where the valley walls are steep, there is still a stone altar set in a grove. That was tended, openly at first, and later in secret, for long after the priests of Rome chanted masses in the church.

In that country the valley is reckoned rich. Life there was good until the Nazis came. Then the Count was shot in his own courtyard, since he was not the type of man to suffer the arrogance of others calmly, and with him Hudun, the head gamekeeper, and the heads of three valley households. Afterwards they took away the young Countess Ana.

But Ivor Kark fled to the hills and our young men joined him. During two years, perhaps a little more, they carried on guerrilla warfare with the invader, just as it happened in those days in all the countries stamped by the iron heel.

But to my country there came no liberation. Where the Nazi had strutted in his pride, the Bear of the north shambled, and stamped into red dust those who defied him. Some fled and some stayed to fight, believing in their innocence that the nations among the free would rise in their behalf.

Ivor Kark and his men, not yet realizing fully the doom come upon us, ventured out of the mountains. For a time it appeared that the valley, being so small a community, might indeed be overlooked. In those few days of freedom Ivor found Dagmar Llov.

Who can describe such a woman as Dagmar with words? She was not beautiful; no, seldom is it that great beauty brings men to their knees. Look at the portraits of your historical charmers, or read what has been written of Cleopatra, of Theodora and the rest. They have something other than beauty, these fateful ones: a flame within them which kindles an answer in all men who look upon them. But their own hearts remain cold.

Dagmar walked with a grace which tore at you, and when she looked at one sidewise. . . . But who can describe such a woman? I can say she had silver, fair hair which reached to her knees, a face with a frost white skin, but I cannot so make you see the Dagmar Llov that was.

Because of his leadership in the underground, Ivor was a hero to us. In addition, he was good to look upon: a tall whip of a man, brown, thin, narrow of waist and loins, and broad of shoulder. He had been a huntsman of the Count's, and walked with a forester's smooth glide. Above his widely set eyes his hair grew in a sharp peak, giving his face a disturbingly wolfish cast. But in his eyes and mouth there was the dedication of a priest.

Being what she was, Dagmar looked upon those eyes and that mouth, and desired to trouble the mold, to see there a difference she had wrought. In some ways Ivor was an innocent, but Dagmar was one who had known much from her cradle.

Also, Ivor was now the great man among us. With the Count gone, the men of the valley looked to him for leadership. Dagmar went to him willingly and we sang her bride song. It was a good time, such as we had not known for years.

Others came back to the valley during those days. Out of the black horror of a Nazi extermination camp crawled a pale, twisted creature, warped in body, perhaps also in mind. She who had once been the Countess Ana came quietly, almost secretly, among us again. One day she had not been there, and the next she was settled in the half-ruinous gate house of the castle with old Mald, who had been with her family long before her own birth.

The Countess Ana had been a woman of edu-

cation before they had taken her away, and she
had not forgotten all she had learned. There was
no doctor in the valley, twenty families could
not have supported one. But the Countess was
versed in the growing of herbs and their healing
uses, and Mald was a midwife. So together they
became the wise women of our people. After a
while we forgot the Countess Ana's deformed
body and ravaged face, and accepted her as we
accepted the crooked firs growing close to the
timberline. Not one of us remembered that she
was yet in years a young woman, with a young
woman's dreams and desires, encased in a hag's
body.

It was late October when our fate came upon
us, up river in a power boat. The new masters
would set in our hills a station from which their
machines could spy upon the outer world they
feared and hated; and to make safe the building
of that station they sent ahead a conqueror's
party. They surprised us and something had
drained out of the valley. So many of our youth
were long since bleached bones that, save for a
handful, perhaps only the number of the fingers
on my two hands, there was no defiance; there
was only a dumb beast's endurance. Within
three days Colonel Andrei Varoff ruled from the
castle as if he had been Count, lord of a tired,
cowed people.

Three men they hauled from their homes and
shot on the first night, but Ivor was not one. He
had been warned and, with the core of his men,
had taken again to the mountains. But he left
Dagmar behind, by her own will.

Mald and the Countess were warned, too.

When Varoff marched his pocket army into the castle, the gate house was deserted; and those who thereafter sought the wise women's aid took another path, up into the black-green of the fir forest and close to a long stone partly buried in the ground within a circle of very old oaks, which had not grown so by chance. There in a game-station hut, those in need could find what they wanted, perhaps more.

Father Hansel had been one of the three Varoff shot out of hand, and there was no longer an open church in the valley. What went on in the oak glade was another matter. First our women drifted there, half ashamed, half defiant, and later they were followed by their men. I do not think the Countess Ana was their priestess. But she knew and condoned. For she had learned many things.

The wise women began to offer more than just comfort of body. It was a queer wild time when men in their despair turned from old belief to older ones, from a god of love and peace, to a god of wrath and vengeance. Old knowledge passed by word of mouth from mother to daughter was recalled by such as Mald, and keenly evaluated by the sharper and better-trained brain of the Countess Ana. I will not say that they called upon Odin and Freya (or those behind those Nordic spirits) or lighted the Beltane Fire. But there was a stirring, as if something long sleeping turned and stretched in its supposed grave.

Dagmar, for all her shrewd egotism (and egotism such as hers is dangerous, for it leads a man or woman to believe that what they wish is right), was a daughter of the valley. She was moved by the old beliefs; and because she had her price, she was convinced that all others had theirs. So at night she went alone to the hut. There she watched until the Countess Ana left. It was she who carried news and a few desperately gained supplies to those in hiding, especially Ivor.

Seeing the hunched figure creep off, Dagmar laughed spitefully, making a secret promise to herself that even a man she might choose to throw away would go to no other woman. But since at present she needed aid and not ill-will, she put that aside.

When the Countess was out of sight, Dagmar went in to Mald and stood in the half-light of the fire, proud and tall, exulting over the other woman in all the sensual strength and grace of her body, as she had over the Countess Ana in her mind.

"I would have what I desire most, Andrei Varoff," she said boldly, speaking with the arrogance of a woman who rules men by their lusts.

"Let him but look on you. You need no help here," returned Mald.

"I cannot come to him easily; he is not one to be met by chance. Give me that which will bring him to me by his own choice."

"You are a wedded wife."

Dagmar laughed shrilly. "What good does a man who must hide ever in a mountain cave do me, Old One? I have slept too long in a cold bed. Let me draw Varoff, and you and the valley will have kin within the enemy's gate."

Mald studied her for a long moment, and Dagmar grew uneasy, for those eyes in age-carved pits seemed to read far too deeply. But, without making any answer in words, Mald began certain preparations. There was a strange chanting, low and soft but long, that night. The words were almost as old as the hills around them, and the air of the hut was thick with the scent of burning herbs.

When it was done Dagmar stood again by the fire, and in her hands she turned and twisted a shining, silken belt. She looped it about her arm beneath her cloak and tugged at the heavy coronet of her braids. The long locks Mald had shorn were not missed. Her teeth showed in white points against her lip as she brought out of her pocket some of those creased slips of paper our conquerors used for money.

Mald shook her head. "Not for coin did I do this," she said harshly. "But if you come to rule here as you desire, remember you are kin."

Dagmar laughed again, more than ever sure of herself. "Be sure that I will, Old One."

Within two days the silken belt was in Varoff's hands, and within five Dagmar was installed in the castle. But in the Colonel she had met her match, for Varoff found her no great novelty. She could not bend him to her will as she had Ivor, who was more sensitive and less guarded. But, being shrewd, Dagmar accepted the situation with surface grace and made no demands.

As for the valley women, they spat after her, and there was hate in their hearts. Who told Ivor I do not know, though it was not the Countess Ana. (She could not wound where she would die

to defend.) But somehow he managed to get a
message to Dagmar, entreating her to come to
him, for he believed she had gone to Varoff to
protect him.

What that message aroused in Dagmar was
contempt and fear: contempt for the man who
would call her to share his harsh exile and fear
that he might break the slender bond she had
with Varoff. She was determined that Ivor must
go. It was very simple, that betrayal, for Ivor
believed in her. He went to his death as easily as
a bullock led to the butcher, in spite of warn-
ings from the Countess Ana and his men.

He slipped down by night to where Dagmar
promised to wait and walked into the hands of
the Colonel's guard. They say he was a long
time dying, for Andrei Varoff had a taste for
such treatment for prisoners when he could
safely indulge it. Dagmar watched him die; that,
too, was part of the Colonel's pleasure. After-
ward there was a strange shadow in her eyes,
although she walked with pride.

It was two months later that she made her
second visit to Mald. But this time there were
two to receive her. Yet in neither look, word, nor
deed, did either show emotion at that meeting; it
was as if they waited. They remained silent, forc-
ing her to declare her purpose.

"I would bear a son." She began as one giving
an order. Only—confronted by those unchang-
ing faces she faltered and lost some of her assurance. She might even have turned and gone had
the Countess Ana not spoken in a cool and even
voice.

"It is well known that Varoff desires a son."

Dagmar responded to that faint encouragement. "True! Let me be the one to bear the child and my influence over him will be complete. Then I can repay—it is true, you frozen faces!" She was aroused by the masks they wore. "You believe that I betrayed Ivor, not knowing the whole of the story. I have very little power over Varoff now. But let me give him a son; then there will be no limit on what I can demand of him—none at all!"

"You shall bear a son; certainly you shall bear a son," replied the Countess Ana. In the security of that promise Dagmar rejoiced, not attending to the finer shades of meaning in the voice which uttered it.

"But what you ask of us takes preparation. You must wait and return when the moon once more waxes. Then we shall do what is to be done!"

Reassured, Dagmar left. As the door of the hut swung shut behind her, the Countess Ana came to stand before the fire, her crooked shape making a blot upon the wall with its shadow.

"She shall have a son, Mald, even as I promised, only whether thereafter she will discover it profitable—"

From within the folds of her coarse peasant blouse, she brought out a packet wrapped in a scrap of fine but brown-stained linen. Unfolding the cloth, she revealed what it guarded: a lock of black hair, stiff and matted with something more than mud. Mald, seeing that and guessing the purpose for which it would be used, laughed. The Countess did not so much as smile.

"There shall be a son, Mald," she repeated, but

her promise was no threat. There was a more subtle note, and in the firelight her eyes gleamed with an eagerness to belie the ruin of her face.

Within two days came the night she had appointed and Dagmar with it. Again there was chanting and things done in secret. When Dagmar left at dawn she smiled a thin smile. Let her but bear a child and they would see, all would see, how she would deal with those who now dared to look crosswise after her and spit upon her footprints! Let such fools take heed!

Shortly thereafter it became known that Dagmar was with child. Varoff could not conceal his joy. During the months which followed he made plans to send her out of the valley, that his son might be born with the best medical care; and he loaded her with gifts. But the inner caution of an often-disappointed man made him keep her prisoner.

Dagmar did not leave the valley. She could not make the rough trip by river and sea. The road over the mountain was but a narrow track, and just before Varoff prepared to leave with her there was such a storm as is seldom seen at that time of year. A landslide blotted out the road. The Colonel cursed and drove his own soldiers and the valley men to dig a way through, but even he realized it could not be cleared in time.

So he was forced to summon Mald. His threats to her were cold and deadly, for he had no illusions concerning the depth of the valley's hatred. But the old woman bore his raving meekly, and he came to believe her broken enough in spirit to be harmless. Thus, though he still suspected her, he brought her to Dagmar and bade her use her skill.

For a night and a day Dagmar lay in labor, and what she suffered must have been very great. But greater still was her determination to be the one to place a living son in the arms of Andrei Varoff.

In the evening the child was born, its thin cry echoing from the walls of the ancient room like the wail of a tormented soul. Dagmar clawed herself up.

"Is it a boy?" she demanded hoarsely.

Mald nodded her white head. "A boy."

"Give him to me and call—"

But there was no need to complete that order for Andrei Varoff was already within the chamber and Dagmar greeted him proudly, the baby in the curve of her arm. As he strode to the bedside she thrust away the swaddling blanket and displayed the tiny body fully. But her eyes were for Varoff rather than for the child she had schemed to make a weapon in her hand.

"Your son—" she began. Then something in Varoff's eyes as he stared down upon the child chilled her as if naked steel, ice cold, had been plunged into her sweating body.

For the first time she looked upon the baby. This was her key, a son for Varoff.

Her scream, thin and high, tore through the storm wind moaning outside the narrow window. Andrei loomed over her as she cowered away from what she read in his eyes, in the twist of his thick lips.

It was Mald who snatched the baby and sped from that room, at a greater speed than her years

might warrant, to be joined by another within a
secret way of the castle. The twisted, limping
figure took the child eagerly into long empty
arms, to hold it tenderly as a long-desired gift.

But neither of the two Mald left were aware of
her flight. What was done there cannot be told
but before the coming of dawn Varoff shot himself.

Where is the magic in all this, besides the
muttering of old women? Just this: when Dagmar demanded a son from the Countess Ana, she
indeed obtained her desire. But the child she
bore had fine black hair growing in a sharp peak
above a wolf cub's face—a face which Andrei
Varoff and Dagmar Kark had excellent reason to
know well. Who fathered Dagmar's child, a man
nigh twelve months dead? And who was its true
mother? Think carefully, my friend.

Not a pretty story, eh? But, you see, old gods
do not tend to be mild when called on to render
justice.

ULLY THE PIPER

THE DALES of High Halleck are many and some are
even forgotten, save by those who live in them.
During the great war with the invaders from
overseas, when the lords of the dales and their
armsmen fought, skulked, prospered or sank in
defeat, there were small places left to a kind of
slumber, overlooked by warriors. There, life
went on as it always had, the dalesmen content
in their islands of safety, letting the rest of the
world roar on as it would.

In such a dale lay Coomb Brackett, a straggle of
houses and farms with no right to the title of
village, though so the indwellers called it. So tall
were the ridges guarding it that few but the wild
shepherds of the crags knew what lay beyond
them, and many of their tales were discounted
by the dalesmen. But there were also ill legends
about those heights that had come down from

the elder days when humankind first pushed
this far north and west. For men were not the
first to settle here, though story said that their
predecessors had worn the outward seeming of
men for convenience, their real aspect being
such that no dalesman would care to look upon
them by morn light.

While those elder ones had withdrawn, seeking a refuge in the Beyond Wilderness, yet at
times they returned on strange pilgrimages. Did
not the dalesmen keep certain feast days—or
nights—when they took offerings up to rocks
which bore queer markings that had not been
chiseled there by wind and weather? The reason
for those offerings no man now living could tell,
but that luck followed their giving was an established fact.

But the dale was good enough for the men of
Coomb Brackett. Its fields were rich, a shallow
river winding through them. Orchards of fruit
flourished and small woodland copses held nut
trees which also bore crops in season. Fat sheep
fed placidly in the uplands, cattle ambled to the
river to drink and went then to graze once more.
Men sowed in spring, harvested in early autumn and lay snug in their homesteads in winter. As they often said to one another, who
wanted more in this life?

They were as plump as their cattle and almost
as slow moving at times. There was little to
plague them, for even the Lord of Fartherdale, to
whom they owed loyalty, had not sent his tithe-
men for a tale of years. There was a rumor that
the lord was dead in the far-off war. Some of the

prudent put aside a folding of woolen or a bolting of linen, well sprinkled with herbs to keep it fresh, against the day when the tithes might be asked again. But for the most part they spun their flax and wool, wove it into stout cloth for their own backs, ate their beef and mutton, drank ale brewed from their barley and wine from their fruit, and thought that trouble was something which struck at others far beyond their protecting heights.

There was only one among them who was not satisfied with things as they comfortably were, because for him there was no comfort. Ully of the hands was not the smallest, nor the youngest of the lads of Coomb Brackett—he was the different one. Longing to be as the rest filled him sometimes with a pain he could hardly bear.

He sat on his small cart and watched the rest off to the feasting on May Day and Harvest Home; and he watched them dance Rings Around following the smoking great roast at Yule—his clever hands folded in upon themselves until the nails bit sorely into the flesh of his palms.

There had been a tree to climb when he was so young he could not rightly recollect what life had been like before that hour. After he fell he had learned what it meant to go hunched of back and useless of leg, able to get from one place to another only by huddling on his cart and pushing it along the ground with two sticks.

He was mender-in-chief for the dale, though he could never mend himself. Aught that was broken was brought to him so that his widowed

mother could sort out the pieces, and then Ully
worked patiently hour by hour to make it whole
again. Sometimes he thought that more than his
body had been broken in that fall, and that
slowly pieces of his spirit were flaking away
with him. For Ully, being chained to his cart,
was active in his mind and had many strange
ideas he never shared with the world.

Only on a night such as this, when it was
midsummer and the youth of the village were
streaming up into the hills to set out first fruit,
new bread, a flagon of milk and another of wine
on the offering rock . . . He did not want to sit
and think his life away! He was young in spirit,
torn by such longings as sometimes made him
want to howl and beat with his fists upon the
ground, or pound the body which imprisoned
him. But for the sake of his mother he never gave
way so, for she would believe him mad, and he
was not that—yet.

He listened to the singing as the company
climbed, giving the rallying call to the all-night
dancing:

> "High Dilly, High Dally,
> Come Lilly, Come Lally!
> Dance for the Ribbons—
> Dance for new Shoes!"

Who would dance so well this night that he
would return by morn's light wearing the new
shoes, she the snood of bright ribbons?

Not Stephen of the mill; he was as heavy-
footed in such frolicking as if he carried one of

the filled flour sacks across his ox-strong shoulders. Not Gretta of the inn, who so wanted to be
graceful. (Ully had seen her in the goose
meadow by the river practicing steps in secret.
She was a kind maid and he wished her as well
as he did any of those he thought of as the
straight people.)

No, this year, as always, it would be Matt of
High Ridge Garth, and Morgana, the smith's
daughter. Ully frowned at the hedge which hid
the upper road from him, crouched low as he
was.

Morgana he knew little of, save that she saw
only what she wished to see and did only what
it pleased her to do. But Matt he disliked, for
Matt was rough of hand and tongue, caring little what he left broken or torn behind his heavily tramped way—whether it was something
which could be mended, or the feelings of
others, which could not. Ully had had to deal
with both kinds of Matt's destruction, and some
he had never been able to put right.

They were still singing.

Ully set his teeth hard upon his lower lip. He
might be small and crooked of body, but he was a
man; and a man did not wail over his hurts. It
was so fine a night he could not bear as yet to go
back to the cottage. The scent of his mother's
garden arose about him, seeming even stronger
in the twilight. He reached within his shirt and
brought out his greatest triumph of mending,
twisted it in his clever fingers and then raised it
to his lips.

The winter before, one of the rare strangers

who ever came over the almost obliterated ridge
road had stopped at the inn. He had brought
news of battles and lords they had never heard
of. Most of Coomb Brackett, even men from the
high garths, had come to listen, though to them it
was more tale than reality.

At last the stranger had pulled out this pipe of
polished wood and had blown sweet notes on it.
Then he had laid it aside as Morgana came to
share his bench; she took it as her just due that
the first smiles of any man were for her. Matt,
jealous of the outsider, had slammed down his
tankard so hard that he had jarred the pipe to the
floor and broken it.

There had been hot words then, and Matt had
sullenly paid the stranger a silver piece. But
Gretta had picked up the pieces and brought
them to Ully, saying wistfully that the music the
stranger had made on it was so sweet she longed
to hear its like again.

Ully had worked hard to put it together and
when it was complete once again he had taken to
blowing an odd note or two. Then he tried even
more, imitating a bird's song, the sleepy murmur
of the river, the wind in the trees. Now he played
the song he had so put together note by note,
combining the many voices of the dale itself.
Hesitatingly he began, then grew more confident. Suddenly he was startled by a clapping of
hands and jerked his head painfully around to
see Gretta by the hedge.

"Play—oh, please play more, Ully! A body
could dance as light as a wind-driven cloud to
music like that."

She took up her full skirt in her hands and pointed her toes. But then Ully saw her smile fade, and he knew well her sorrow, the clumsy body which would not obey the lightness of mind. In a moment she was smiling again and ran to him, holding out her work-callused hand.

"Such music we have never had, Ully. You must come along and play for us tonight!"

He shrank back, shaking his head, but Gretta coaxed. Then she called over her shoulder.

"Stephen, Will! Come help me with Ully, he can pipe sweeter than any bird in the bush. Let him play for our dancing tonight and we shall be as well served as they say the old ones were with their golden pipes!"

Somehow Ully could not refuse them, and Stephen and Will pushed the cart up to the highest meadow where the token feast had been already spread on the offering rock and the fire flamed high. There Ully set pipe to lips and played.

But there were some not so well pleased at his coming. Morgana, having halted in the dance not far away, saw him and cried out so that Matt stepped protectingly before her.

"Ah, it's only crooked Ully," she cried spitefully. "I had thought it some one of the monsters out of the old tales crawled up from the woods to spy on us." And she gave an exaggerated shiver, clinging to Matt's arm.

"Ully?" Matt laughed. "Why does Ully crawl here, having no feet to dance upon? Why stare at his betters? And where did you get that pipe, little man?" He snatched at the pipe in Ully's hands. "It looks to me like the one I had to pay a round piece for when it was broken. Give it here now; for if it is the same, it belongs to me!"

Ully tried to hold on to the pipe, but Matt's strength was by far the greater. The resting dancers had gathered close to the offering rock where they were opening their own baskets and bags to share the midnight feast. There were none to see what chanced here in the shadow. Matt held up the pipe in triumph.

"Good as new, and worth surely a silver piece again. Samkin the peddler will give me that and I shall not be out of the pocket at all."

"My pipe!" Ully struggled to get it but Matt held it well out of his reach.

"My pipe, crooked man! I had to pay for it, didn't I? Mine to do with as I will."

Helpless anger worked in Ully as he tried to raise himself higher, but his movements only set the wheels of the cart moving and he began to roll down slope of the meadow backwards. Morgana cried out and moved as if to stop him. But Matt, laughing, caught her back.

"Let him go, he will come to no harm. And he has no place here now, has he? Did he not even frighten you?"

He put the pipe into his tunic and threw an arm about her waist, leading her back to the feast. Halfway they met Gretta.

"Where is Ully?"

Matt shrugged. "He is gone."

"Gone? But it is a long way back to the village and he—" She began to run down the slope of the hill calling, "Ully! Ully!"

The runaway cart had not gone that way, but in another direction, bumping and bouncing towards the small wood which encircled half the high meadow, its green arms held out to embrace the open land.

Ully crouched low, afraid to move, afraid to try to catch at any of the shrubs or low hanging branches as he swept by, lest he be pulled off to lie helpless on the ground.

In and out among the trees spun the cart, and Ully began to wonder why it had not upset, or run against a trunk, or caught in some vine. It was almost as if it were being guided. When he tried to turn and look to the fore, he could see nothing but the dark wood.

Then with a rush, the cart burst once more into the open. No fire blazed here, but the moon seemed to hang oddly bright and full just above, as if it were a fixed lamp. Heartened somehow, Ully dared to reach out and catch at a tuft of thick grass, a vine runner, and pulled the cart around so that he no longer faced the wood through which he had come, but rather an open glade where the grass grew short and thick as if it were mown. Around was a wall of flowers and bushes, while in the middle was a ring of stones, each taller than Ully, and so blazingly white in the moonlight that they might have been upright torches.

Ully's heart ceased to pound so hard. The peace and beauty of the place soothed him as if soft fingers stroked his damp face and ordered his tousled hair. His hands resting on his shrunken knees twitched, he so wanted his pipe.

But there was no pipe. Softly Ully began to hum his tune of the dale: bird song, water ripple, wind. Then his hum became a whistle. It seemed to him that all the beauty he had ever dreamed of was gathered here, just as he had fit together broken bits with his hands.

Great silvery moths came out of nowhere and sailed in and out among the candle pillars, as if they were weaving some unseen fabric, netting a spell. Hesitatingly Ully held out one hand and one of the moths broke from the rest and lit fearlessly on his wrist, fanning wings which might have been tipped with stardust for the many points of glitter there. It was so light he was hardly aware that it rested so, save that he saw it. Then it took to the air again.

Ully wiped the hand across his forehead, sweeping back a loose lock of hair, and as he did so . . .

The moths were gone; beside each pillar stood a woman. Small and slight indeed they were, hardly taller than a young child of Ully's kin, but these were truly women, for they were dressed only in their long hair. The bodies revealed as they moved were so perfectly formed that Ully knew he had never seen real beauty before. They did not look at him, but glided on their small bare feet in and out among the pillars, weaving their spell even as the moths had done. At times they paused, gathering up their hair with their two hands, to hold it well away from their bodies and shake it. It seemed to Ully that when they did so there was a shifting of glittering motes carried along in a small cloud moving away from the glade, though he did not turn his eyes to follow it.

Though none of them spoke, he knew what they wanted of him and he whistled his song of the dale. He must truly be asleep and dreaming, or else in that wild dash downslope he had fallen from the cart and suffered a knock from which this vision was born. But dream or hurt, he would hold to it as long as he could. This—this was such happiness as he had never known.

At last their dance grew slower and slower, until they halted, each standing with one hand upon a pillar side. Then they were gone; only the moths fluttered once again in the dimming light.

Ully was aware that his body ached, that his lips and mouth were dry and that all the weight of fatigue had suddenly fallen on him. But still he cried out against its ending.

There was movement by the pillar directly facing him and someone came farther into the pale light of new dawn. She stood before him, and for the last time she gathered up her hair in both hands, holding it out shoulder high. Once, twice, thrice, she shook it. But this time there were no glittering motes. Rather he was struck in the face by a blast of icy air, knocked from his cart so his head rapped against the ground, dazing him.

He did not know how long it was before he tried to move. But he did struggle up, braced on his forearms. Struggle—he writhed and fought for balance.

Ully who could not move his shriveled legs, nor straighten his back—why—he was straight!

He was as straight as Stephen, as Matt! If this were a dream . . .

He arched up, looked for the woman to babble questions, thanks, he knew not what. But there was no one by the pillar. Hardly daring to trust the fact that he was no longer bowed into a broken thing, he crawled, feeling strength flow into him with every move, to the foot of the pillar. He used that to draw himself to his feet, to stand again!

His clothes were too confining for his new body. He tore them away. Then he was erect, the pillar at his back and the dawn wind fresh on his body. Still keeping his hold on the white stone, he took small cautious steps, circling his support. His feet moved and were firm under him; he did not fall.

Ully threw back his head and cried his joy aloud. Then he saw the glint of something lying in the center of the pillar circle and he edged forward. A sod of green turf was half up-rooted, and protruding from it was a pipe. But such a pipe! He had thought the one he mended was fine; this was such as a high lord might treasure!

He picked it loose of the earth, fearing it might well disappear out of his very fingers. Then he put it to his lips and played his thanks to what, or who, had been there in the night; he played with all the joy in him.

So playing he went home, walking with care at first because it was so new to him. He went by back ways until he reached the cottage and his mother. She, poor woman, was weeping. They had feared him lost when he had vanished from the meadow and Gretta had aroused the others to

search for him without result. When she first
looked at this new Ully his mother judged him a
spirit from the dead, until he reassured her.

All Coomb Brackett marveled at his story.
Some of the oldest nodded knowingly, spoke of
ancient legends of the old ones who had once
dwelt in the dales, and how it was that they
could grant blessings to those they favored. They
pointed out symbols on the pipe which were not
unlike those of the tribute rock. Then the
younger men spoke of going to the pillar glade to
hunt for treasure. But Ully grew wroth and they
respected him as one set apart by what had
happened, and agreed it was best not to trouble
those they knew so little of.

It would seem that Ully had brought back
more than straight legs and a pipe. For that was a
good year in the dale. The harvest was the richest
in memory, and there were no ill happenings.
Ully, now on his two feet, traveled to the farthest
homestead to mend and play, for the pipe never
left him. And it was true that when they listened
to it the feet of all grew lighter as did their hearts,
and any dancer more skillful.

But inside Matt there was no rest. Now he
was no longer first among the youth; Ully was
more listened to. He began to talk himself, hint-
ing dire things about gifts from unknown
sources, and a few listened, those who are always discontent to see another prosper. Among
them was Morgana, for she was no longer so
courted. Even Gretta nowadays was sometimes
partnered before her. And one day she broke
through Matt's grumbling shortly.

"What one man can do, surely another can

also. Why do you keep muttering about Ully's fortune? Harvest Eve comes soon and those old ones are supposed then to come again to view the wealth of the fields and take their due. Go to Ully's pillars and play; they may be grateful again!''

Matt had been practicing on the pipe he had taken from Ully, and he did well enough with the rounds and the lays the villagers had once liked; though the few times he had tried to play Ully's own song the notes had come sourly, off key.

The more Matt considered Morgana's suggestion, the better it seemed, and the old thought of treasure clung in his mind. There could be deals with the old ones if a man were shrewd. Ully was a simple fellow who had not known how to handle such. His thoughts grew ambitious.

So when the feast came Matt lagged behind the rest and turned aside to take a brambly way he judged would bring him to Ully's oft-described ring of pillars. Leaving much of his shirt hanging in tatters on the briers and his skin redstriped by thorns, he came at last into the glade.

There were the pillars right enough, but they were not bright and white and torchlike. Instead, each seemed to squat direfully in a mass of shadow which flowed about their bases as if something unpleasant undulated there. But Matt dropped down beneath one of the trees to wait. He saw no moths, though there were vague flutterings about the crowns of the pillars. At last, thinking Ully fashioned out of his own imagina-

tion much of his story, Matt decided to try one
experiment before going back to the feasting villagers to proclaim just how much a liar his rival
was.

But the notes he blew on his pipe were shrill
squeaks; and when he would have left, he found
to his horror and dismay that he could not move,
his legs were locked to the ground as Ully's had
once been. Nor could he lower the pipe from his
lips, but was compelled by a will outside his
own to keep up that doeful, sorry wailing. His
body ached, his mouth was dry, and fear was laid
as a lash upon him. He saw things around those
pillars.

He would close his eyes! But again he could
not, but must pipe and watch, until he was close
to the brink of madness. Then his leaden arms
fell, the pipe spun away from his lax fingers, and
he was dimly aware the dawn had come.

From the pillar before him sped a great bloated
thing with an angry buzzing—such a fly as he
had seen gather to drink the blood spilled at a
butchering—yet this was greater than six of
those put into one.

It flew straight into his face, stinging him. He
tried to beat it away, but could only manage to
crawl on his hands and knees; the fly continued
to buzz about him as a sheep dog might herd a
straggler.

Somehow Matt finally struggled to his feet,
but it was long before he could walk erect. For
many days his face was so swollen that he would
not show it in the village, nor would he ever tell
what had happened to him.

But for many a year thereafter Ully's pipe led
the people of Coomb Brackett to their feasting
and played for their dancing. Sometimes, it was
known, he slipped away by himself to the place
of pillars and there played for other ears, such as
did not side mortal heads.

TOYS OF TAMISAN

I

"She is certified by the Foostmam, Lord Starrex, a true action dreamer to the tenth power!"

Jabis was being too eager, or almost so; he was pushing too much. Tamisan sneered mentally, keeping her face carefully blank, though she took quick glances about from beneath half-closed eyelids. This sale very much concerned herself, since she was the product being discussed, but she had nothing to say in the matter.

She supposed this was a typical sky tower. It seemed to float, since its supports were so slender and well concealed, lifting it high above Ty-Kry. However, none of the windows gave on real sky. Each framed a very different landscape, illustrating, she guessed, other planet scenes; perhaps some were dream remembered or inspired.

There was a living lambil-grass carpet around the easirest on which the owner half lay and half sat. But Jabis had not even been offered a pull-down wall seat, and the two other men in attendance on Lord Starrex stood also. They were real men and not androids, which placed the owner in the multi-credit class. One, Tamisan thought, was a bodyguard, and the other, who was younger and thinner, with a dissatisfied mouth, had on clothing nearly equal to that of the man on the easirest, but with a shade of difference which meant a lesser place in the household.

Tamisan catalogued what she could see and filed it away for future reference. Most dreamers did not observe much of the world about them, they were too enmeshed in their own creations to care for reality. Tamisan frowned. She *was* a dreamer. Jabis, and the Foostmam could prove that. The lounger on the easirest could prove it if he paid Jabis' price. But she was also something more; Tamisan herself was not quite sure what. That there was a difference in her she had had mother wit enough to conceal since she had first been aware that the others in the Foostmam's Hive were not able to come cleanly out of their dreams into the here and now. Why, some of them had to be fed, clothed, cared for as if they were not aware they had any bodies!

"Action dreamer." Lord Starrex shifted his shoulder against the padding which immediately accommodated itself to his stirring to give him maximum comfort. "Action dreaming is a little childish."

Tamisan's control held. She felt inside her a small flare of anger. Childish was it? She would like to show him just how childish a dream she could spin to enmesh a client. But Jabis was not in the least moved by that derogatory remark from a possible purchaser, it was in his eyes only a logical bargaining move.

"If you wish an E dreamer . . ." He shrugged. "But your demand to the Hive specified an A."

He was daring to be a little abrupt. Was he so sure of this lord as all that, Tamisan wondered. He must have some inside information which allowed him to be so confident, for Jabis could cringe and belly-down in awe as the lowest beggar if he thought such a gesture needful to gain a credit or two.

"Kas, this is your idea; what is she worth?" Starrex asked indifferently.

The younger of his companions moved forward a step or two; he was the reason for her being here. He was Lord Kas, cousin to the owner of all this magnificence, though certainly not, Tamisan had already deduced, with any authority in the household. But the fact that Starrex lay in the easirest was not dictated by indolence, but rather by what was hidden by the fas-silk lap robe concealing half his body. A man who might not walk straight again could find pleasure in the abilities of an action dreamer.

"She has a ten-point rating," Kas reminded the other.

The black brows which gave a stern set to Starrex's features arose a trifle. "Is that so?"

Jabis was quick to take advantage. "It is so,

Lord Starrex. Of all this year's swarm, she rated
the highest. It was—is—the reason why we make
this offer to your lordship."

"I do not pay for reports only," returned Starrex.

Jabis was not to be ruffled. "A point ten, my
lord, does not give demonstrations. As you
know, the Hive accrediting can not be forged. It
is only that I have urgent business in Brok and
must leave for there, that I am selling her at all. I
have had an offer from the Footsmam herself to
retain this one for lease outs."

Tamisan, had she had anything to wager, or
someone with whom to wager it, would have set
this winning of this bout with her uncle. Uncle?
To Tamisan's thinking she had no blood tie with
this small insect of a man—with his wrinkled
face, his never-still eyes and his thin hands with
their half crooked fingers always reminding her
of claws outstretched to grab. Surely her mother
must have been very unlike Uncle Jabis, or else
how could her father ever have seen aught worth
bedding (not for just one night but for half a
year) in her.

Not for the first time her thoughts were on the
riddle of her parents. Her mother had not been a
dreamer—though she had had a sister who had
regrettably (for the sake of the family fortune)
died in the Hive during adolescent stimulation
as an E dreamer. Her father had been from off
world—an alien, though humanoid enough to
crossbreed. He had disappeared again off world
when his desire for star roving had become too
strong to master. Had it not been that she had

early shown dreamer talent Uncle Jabis and the
rest of the greedy Yeska clan would never have
taken any thought of her after her mother had
died of the blue plague.

She was crossbred and had intelligence
enough to guess early that that had given her
the difference between her powers and those of
others in the Hive. The ability to dream was an
inborn talent. For those of low power it was a
withdrawal from the world, and those dreamers
were largely useless. But the others, who could
project dreams to include others through linkage, brought high prices, according to the
strength and stability of their creations. E
dreamers, who created erotic and lascivious
otherworlds once were rated more highly than
action dreamers. But of late years the swing had
been in the opposite direction, though how long
that might hold no one could guess. Those lucky
enough to have an A dreamer to sell were pushing their wares speedily lest the market decline.

Tamisan's hidden talent was that she herself
was never as completely lost in the dream world
as those she conveyed to it. Also (and this she
had discovered very recently and hugged that
discovery to her) she could in a measure control
the linkage so she was not a powerless prisoner
forced to dream at another's desire.

She considered what she knew concerning
Lord Starrex. That Jabis would sell her to the
owner of one of the sky towers had been clear
from the first, and naturally he would select
what he thought would be the best bargain. But,
though rumors wafted through the Hive, Tami-

san believed that much of their news of the outer worlds was inaccurate and garbled. Dreamers were roofed and walled from any real meeting with every day life, their talents feverishly fed and fostered by long sessions with tri-dee projectors and information tapes.

Starrex, unlike most of his class, had been a doer. He had broken the pattern of caste by going off world on lengthy trips. It was only after some mysterious accident had crippled him that he became a recluse, supposedly hiding a maimed body. He did not seem like the others who had come to the Hive seeking wares. Of course, it had been Lord Kas who had summoned them here.

Stretched out on the easirest with that cover of fabulous silk across most of his body, he was hard to judge. She thought that standing he would top Jabis, and he seemed to be well muscled, more like his guard than his cousin.

He had a face unusual in its planes, broad across the forehead and cheek bones, then slimming to a strong chin which narrowed to give his head a vaguely wedge-shaped line. He was dark skinned, almost as dark as a spacecrewman. His black hair was cut very short so that it was a tight velvet cap, in contrast to the longer strands of his cousin.

His lutrax tunic of a coppery rust shade, was of rich material but less ornamented than that of the younger man. Its sleeves were wide and loose, and now and then he ran his hands up his arms, pushing the fabric away from his skin. He wore only a single jewel, a koros stone set in an earring as a drop which dangled forward against his jaw line.

Tamisan did not consider him handsome, but there was something arresting about him. Perhaps it was his air of arrogant assurance, as if in all his life he had never had his wishes crossed. But he had not met Jabis before, and perhaps now even Lord Starrex would have something to learn.

Twisting and turning, indignant and persuasive, using every trick in a very considerable training for dealing and under-dealing, Jabis bargained. He appealed to gods and demons to witness his disinterested desire to please, his despair at being misunderstood. It was quite a notable act and Tamisan stored up some of the choicer bits in her mental reservoir for the making of dreams. It was far more stimulating to watch than a tri-dee, and she wondered why this living drama material was not made available to the Hive. Perhaps, the Foostmam and her assistants feared it, along with any other shred of reality, which might awaken the dreamers from their conditioned absorption in their own creations.

For an instant or two she wondered if Lord Starrex was not enjoying it, too. There was a kind of weariness in his face which suggested boredom, though that was normal for anyone wanting a personal dreamer. Then, suddenly, as if he were tired of it all, he interrupted one of Jabis' more impassioned pleas for celestial understanding of his need for receiving just dues with a single sentence.

"I tire, fellow; take your price and go." He closed his eyes in dismissal.

It was the guard who drew a credit plaque

from his belt, swung a long arm over the back of
the easirest for Lord Starrex to plant a thumb on
its surface to certify payment, and then tossed it
to Jabis. It fell to the floor, so the small man had
to scrabble for it with his fingers. Tamisan saw
the look in his darting eyes. Jabis had little liking
for Lord Starrex, which did not mean, of course,
that he disdained the credit plaque he had to
stoop to catch up.

He did not give a glance to Tamisan as he
bowed himself out. She was left standing as if
she were an android. It was Lord Kas who stepped forward and touched her lightly on the arm
as if he thought she needed guidance.

"Come," he said, and his fingers about her
wrist drew her after him. The Lord Starrex took
no notice of his new possession.

"What is your name?" Lord Kas spoke slowly,
emphasizing each word, as if he needed to do
so to pierce some veil between them. Tamisan
guessed that he had had contact with a lower
rated dreamer, one who was always bemused in
the real world. Caution suggested that she allow
him to believe she was in a similar daze. So she
raised her head slowly and looked at him, trying
to give the appearance of one finding it difficult
to focus.

"Tamisan," she answered after a lengthy
pause. "I be Tamisan."

"Tamisan, that is a pretty name," he said as
one would address a dull-minded child. "I am
Lord Kas. I am your friend."

But Tamisan, sensitive to shades of voice,
thought she had done well in playing bemused.

Whatever Kas might be, he was not her friend, at least not unless it served his purpose.

"These rooms are yours." He had escorted her down a hall to a far door where he passed his hand over the surface in a pattern to break a light lock. Then his grip on her wrist brought her into a high-ceilinged room. There were no windows to interrupt its curve of wall; the place was oval in shape. The center descended in a series of wide, shallow steps to a pool where a small fountain raised a perfumed mist to patter back into a bone-white basin. On the steps were a number of cushions and soft lie-ons, of many delicate shades of blue and green. The oval walls were draped with a shimmer of zidex webbing of pale gray covered with whirls and lines of the palest green.

A great deal of care had gone into the making and furnishing of the room. Perhaps Tamisan was only the latest in a series of dreamers, for this was truly the rest place, raised to a point of luxury unknown even in the Hive, for a dreamer.

A strip of the web tapestry along the wall was raised and a personal-care android entered. The head was only an oval ball with faceted eye-plates and hearing sensors to break its surface; its unclothed, humanoid form was ivory-white.

"This is Porpae," Kas told her. "She will watch over you."

My guard, Tamisan thought. That the care the android would give her would be unceasing and of the best, she did not doubt, any more than that ivory being would stand between her and any hope of freedom.

"If you have any wish, tell it to Porpae." Kas dropped his hold on her arm and turned to the door. "When Lord Starrex wishes to dream, he will send for you."

"I am at his command," she mumbled; it was the proper response.

She watched Kas leave and then looked to Porpae. Tamisan had cause to believe that the android was programmed to record her every move. But would anyone here believe that a dreamer had any desire to be free? A dreamer wished only to dream; it was her life, her entire life. To leave a place which did all to foster such a life—that would be akin to self-killing, something a certified dreamer could not think on.

"I hunger," She told the android. "I would eat."

"Food comes." Porpae went to the wall, swept aside the web once more, to display a series of buttons she pressed in a complicated manner.

When the food did arrive in a closed tray with the viands each in their own hot or cold compartment, Tamisan ate. She recognized the usual dishes of a dreamer's diet, but they were better cooked and more tastily served than in the Hive. She ate, she made use of the bathing place Porpae guided her to behind another wall web and she slept easily and without stirring on the cushions beside the pool where the faint play of the water lulled her.

Time had very little meaning in the oval room. She ate, slept, bathed and looked at the tri-dees she asked Porpae to supply. Had she been as the others from the Hive, this existence would have

been ideal. But instead, when there was no call
to display her art, she grew restless. She was a
prisoner here and none of the other inhabitants
of the sky tower seemed aware of her.

There was one thing she could do, Tamisan
decided upon her second waking. A dreamer
was allowed, no, required, to study the personality of the master she must serve, if she were a
private dreamer and not a leasee of the Hive. She
had a right now to ask for tapes concerning Starrex. In fact it might be considered odd if she did
not, and accordingly she called for those. Thus
she learned something of Starrex and his household.

Kas had had his personal fortune wiped out by
some catastrophe when he was a child. He had
been in a manner adopted by Starrex's father, the
head of their clan, and, since Starrex's injuries,
had acted in some fashion as his deputy. The
guard was Ulfilas, an off-world mercenary, Starrex had brought back from one of his star voy-
ages.

But Starrex, save for a handful of bare facts,
remained an enigma. That he had any human
responses to others, Tamisan began to doubt. He
had gone seeking change off world, but what he
might have found there had not cured his eternal
weariness of life. His personal recordings were
meager. She now believed that to him any one of
his household was only a tool to be used, or
swept from his path and ignored. He was unmar-
ried and such feminine companionship as he
had languidly attached to his household (and
that more by the effort of the woman involved

than through any direct action on his part) did not last long. In fact, he was so encased in a shell of indifference that Tamisan wondered if there was any longer a real man within that outer covering.

She began to speculate as to why he had allowed Kas to bring her as an addition to his belongings. To make the best use of a dreamer the owner must be ready to partake, and what she read in these tapes suggested that Starrex's indifference would raise a barrier to any real dreaming.

The more Tamisan learned in this negative fashion, the more it seemed a challenge. She lay beside the pool in deep thought, though that thought strayed even more than she herself guessed from the rigid mental exercises used by a point-ten dreamer. To deliver a dream which would captivate Starrex was indeed a challenge. He wanted action, but her training, acute as it had been, was not enough to entice him. Therefore, her action must be able to take a novel turn.

This was an age of over-sophistication, when star travel was a fact; and by the tapes, though they were not detailed as to what Starrex had done off world, the lord had experienced much of the reality of his time.

So he must be served the unknown. She had read nothing in the tapes to suggest that Starrex had sadistic or perverted tendencies, and she knew that if he were to be reached in such a fashion she was not the one to do it. Also, Kas would have stated such a requirement at the Hive.

There were many rolls of history on which one could draw, but those had also been mined and remined. The future had been over-used, frayed. Tamisan's dark brows drew together above her closed eyes. It was trite; everything she thought of was trite! Why did she care anyway? She did not even know why it had become so strong a drive to build a dream that, when she was called upon to deliver it, would shake Starrex out of his shell—to prove to him that she was worth her rating. Maybe it was partly because he had made no move to send for her and try to prove her powers; his indifference suggesting that he thought she had nothing to offer.

She had the right to call upon the full library of tapes from the Hive, and it was the most complete in the star lanes. Why, ships were sent out for no other reason than to bring back new knowledge to feed the imaginations of the dreamers!

History—her mind kept returning to the past. Though it was too threadbare for her purposes. History—what was history? It was a series of events, actions by individuals or nations. Actions had results. Tamisan sat up among her cushions. *Results of action!* Sometimes there were far-reaching results from a single action: the death of a ruler, the outcome of one battle, the landing of a star ship or its failure to land. *So . . .*

Her flicker of an idea became solid. History could have had many roads to travel beside the one already known. Now, could she make use of that? Why, it had innumerable possibilities. Tamisan's hands clenched the robe lying across her knees. She would have to study. If Starrex only gave her more time . . . She no longer resented his indifference. She would need every minute it was prolonged.

"Porpae!"

The android materialized from behind the web.

"I must have certain tapes from the Hive." Tamisan hesitated. In spite of the spur of impatience she must build smoothly and surely. "A message to the Foostmam: send to Tamisan n' Starrex the rolls of the history of Ty-Kry for the past five hundred years."

It was the history of the single city which based this sky tower. She would begin small, but she could test and retest her idea. Today it would be a single city, tomorrow a world, and then— who knows?—perhaps a solar system. She reined in her excitement. There was much to do; she needed a note recorder, and time. But by The Four Breasts of Vlasta—*if* she could do it!

It would seem she would have time, though always at the back of Tamisan's mind was the small spark of fear that at any moment the summons to Starrex might come. But the tapes arrived from the Hive and the recorder, so that she swung from one to the other, taking notes from what she learned. After the tapes had been returned, she studied those notes feverishly. Now her idea meant more to her than just a device to amuse a difficult master, it absorbed her utterly, as if she were a low-grade dreamer caught in one of her own creations.

When Tamisan realized the danger of this, she

broke with her studies and turned back to the
household tapes to learn again what she could of
Starrex.

But she was again running through her notes
when at last the summons came. How long she
had been in Starrex's tower she did not know, for
the days and nights in the oval room were all
alike. Only Porpae's watchfulness had kept her
to a routine of eating and rest.

It was the Lord Kas who came for her, and she
had just time to remember her role of bemused
dreamer as he entered.

"You are well, happy?" he used the conventional greeting.

"I enjoy the good life."

"It is the Lord Starrex's wish that he enter a
dream." Kas reached for her hand and she allowed his touch. "The Lord Starrex demands
much; offer him your best, dreamer." He might
have been warning her.

"A dreamer dreams," she answered him vaguely. "What is dreamed can be shared."

"True, but the Lord Starrex is hard to please.
Do your best for him, dreamer."

She did not answer, and he drew her on, out of
the room to a grav shaft and down that to a lower
level. The room into which they finally went had
the apparatus very familiar to her: a couch for the
dreamer, the second for the sharer with the
linkage machine between. But here there was a
third couch; Tamisan looked at it in surprise.

"Two dream, not three."

Kas shook his head. "It is the Lord Starrex's
will that another share also. The linkage is of a

new model, very powerful. It has been well
tested.''

Who would be that third? Ulfilas? Was it that
Lord Starrex thought he must take his personal
guard into a dream with him?

The door swung open again and Lord Starrex
entered. He walked stiffly, one leg swinging
wide as if he could not bend the knee nor control the muscles, and he leaned heavily on an
android. As the servant lowered him onto the
couch he did not look at Tamisan but nodded
curtly to Kas.

"Take your place also," he ordered.

Did Starrex fear the dream state and want his
cousin as a check because Kas had plainly
dreamed before?

Then Starrex did turn to her as he reached for
the dream crown, copying the motion by which
she settled her own circlet on her head.

"Let us see what you can offer." There was a
shadow of hostility in his voice, a challenge to
produce something which he did not believe she
could.

II

She must not allow herself to think of Starrex
now, but only of her dream. She must create and
have no doubt that her creation would be as
perfect as her hopes. Tamisan closed her eyes,
firmed her will, drew into her imagination all
the threads of the studies' spinning and began
the weaving of a dream.

For a moment, perhaps two fingers' count of moments, this was like the beginning of any dream and then. . . .

She was not looking on, watching intently and critically, as she spun with dexterity. No, it was rather as if that web suddenly became real and she was caught tightly in it, even as a blue-winged drotail might be enmeshed in a fess-spider's deadly curtain.

This was no dreaming such as Tamisan had ever known before, and panic gripped so harshly in her throat and chest that she might have screamed, save that she had no voice left. She fell down and down from a point above, to strike among bushes which took some of her weight, but with an impact which left her bruised and half senseless. She lay unmoving, gasping, her eyes closed, fearing to open them to see that she was indeed caught in a wild nightmare and not properly dreaming.

As she lay there, she came slowly out of her dazed bewilderment and tried for control, not only over her fears, but also over her dreaming powers. Then she opened her eyes cautiously.

An arch of sky was overhead, pallidly green, with traces of thin, gray cloud like long, clutching fingers. It would have been as real as any sky might be, did she walk under it in her own time and world. *My own time and world!*

She thought of the idea she had built upon to astound Starrex; her wits quickened. Had the fact that she had worked with a new theory, trying to bring a twist to dreaming which might pierce the indifference of a bored man, precipitated *this*?

Tamisan sat up, wincing at the protest of her bruises, to look about her. Her vantage point was the crest of a small knob of earth. The land about her was no wilderness. The turf was smooth and cropped, and here and there were outcrops of rock cleverly carved and clothed with flowering vines. Other rocks were starkly bare, brooding. All faced downslope to a wall.

These forms varied from vaguely acceptable humanoid shapes to grotesque monsters. Tamisan decided that she liked the aspect of none when she studied them more closely. These were not of her imagining.

Beyond the wall began a cluster of buildings. Since she was used to seeing the sky towers and the lesser, if more substantial structures, beneath those, these looked unusually squat and heavy. The tallest she could see was no more than three stories high. Men did not build to the stars here; they hugged the earth closely.

But where was here? It was not her dream. Tamisan closed her eyes and concentrated on the beginnings of her planned dream. They had been about to go into another world, born of her imagining, but not this. Her basic idea had been simple enough, if not one which had been used, to her knowledge, by any dreamer before her. It all hinged on the idea that the past history of her world had been altered many times during its flow. She had taken three key points of alteration and studied what might have resulted had those been given the opposite decision by fate.

Now, keeping her eyes firmly closed against this seeming reality into which she had fallen,

Tamisan concentrated with fierce intentness upon her chosen points.

"The Welcome of the Over-queen Ahta." She recited the first.

What would have happened if the first star ship on its landing had not been accepted as a supernatural event, and the small kingdom in which it had touched earth had not accepted its crew as godlings, but had greeted them instead with those poisoned darts the spacemen had later seen used? That was her first decision.

"The loss of the *Wanderer*." That was the second.

It had been a colony ship driven far from its assigned course by computer failure, so that it had to make a landing here or its passengers would die. If that failure had not occurred and the *Wanderer* landed to start an unplanned colony, what would have come to pass?

"The death of Sylt the Sweet-Tongued before he reached the Altar of Ictio."

That prophet might never have arisen to ruthless power, leading to a blood-crazed insurrection from temple to temple, setting darkness on three quarters of this world.

She had chosen those points, but she had not even been sure that one might not have canceled out another. Sylt had led the rebellion against the colonists from the *Wanderer*. If the welcome had not occurred . . . Tamisan could not be sure, she had only tried to find a pattern of events and then envision a modern world stemming from those changes.

She opened her eyes again. This was not her

imagined world. Nor did one in a dream rub bruises, sit on damp sod, feel wind pull at them, and allow the first patter of rain to wet hair and robe. She put both hands to her head. *What of the dream crown?*

Her fingers found a weaving of metal, but there were no cords from it. For the first time she remembered that she had been linked with Starrex and Kas when this happened.

Tamisan got to her feet to look around, half expecting to see the other two somewhere near; but she was alone and the rain was falling heavier. There was a roofed space near the wall and Tamisan hurried for it.

Three twisted pillars supported a small dome of roof. There were no walls and she huddled in the very center, trying to escape the wind-borne moisture. She could not keep pushing away the feeling that this was no dream but true reality.

If—if one could dream true. Tamisan fought panic and tried to examine the possibilities. *Had* she somehow landed in a Ty-Kry which might have existed had her three checkpoints actually been the decisions she envisioned? If so, could one get back by simply visioning them in reverse?

She shut her eyes and concentrated.

There was a sensation of stomach-turning giddiness. She swung out, to be jerked back, swung out, to return once more. Shaking with nausea, Tamisan stopped trying. She shuddered, opening her eyes to the rain. Then again she strove to understand what had happened. That swing had in it some of the sensation of dream breaking, which meant that she was in a dream. But it was just as apparent that she had been held prisoner here. *How? And why?* Her eyes narrowed a little, though she was looking inward, not at the rain-misted garden before her. *By whom?*

Suppose—suppose one or both of those who had prepared to share my dream had also come into this place, though not right here—then I must find them. We must return together or the missing one will anchor the others. Find them—and now!

For the first time she looked down at the garment clinging damply to her slender body. It was not the gray slip of a dreamer, for it was long, brushing her ankles. And in color it was a dusky violet, a shade she found strangely pleasing and right.

From its hem to her knees there was a border of intricate embroidery so entwined and ornate that she found it hard to define in any detail. Though, oddly enough, it seemed the longer she studied it, the more it appeared to be not threads on cloth, but words on a page of manuscript, such as she had viewed in the ancient history video tapes. The threads were a metallic green and silver, with only a few minor touches of a lighter shade of violet.

Around her waist was a belt of silver links, clasped by a broad buckle of the same metal set with purple stones. This supported a pouch with a clasped top. The dress or robe was laced from the belt to her throat with silver cords run through metal eyelets in the material. Her sleeves were long and full, though from the elbow down they were slit into four parts, those fluttering away from her arms when she raised them to loosen the crown.

What she brought away from her head was not the familiar skull cap made to fit over her cropped hair, rather it was a circlet of silver with inner wires or strips rising to close in a conical point to add a foot or more on her height. On that point was a beautifully fashioned flying thing, its wings a little lifted as if to take off, the glitter of tiny jewels marking its eyes.

So was it made that, as she turned the crown around, its long neck changed position and the wings moved a fraction. Thus at first she was almost startled enough to drop the circlet, thinking it might be alive.

But the whole she recognized from one of the history tapes. The bird was the flacar of Olava. Wearing it so meant that she was a Mouth, a Mouth of Olava, part priestess, part sorceress and, oddly enough, part entertainer. But fortune had favored her in this; a Mouth of Olava might wander anywhere without question, search, and seem merely to be about her normal business.

Tamisan ran her hand over her head before she replaced the crown. Her fingers did not find the bristly stubble of a dreamer, but rather soft, mist-dampened strands which curled down long enough to brush her forehead and tuft at the nape of her neck.

She had imagined garments for herself in dreams, of course. But this time she had not provided herself with such, and so the fact that

she stood as a Mouth of Olava was not of her
willing. But Olava was part of the time of the
Over-queen's rule. Had she somehow swept herself back in time? The sooner she found knowledge of where and when she was, the better.

The rain was slackening and Tamisan moved
out from under the dome. She bunched up her
robe in both hands to climb back up the slope. At
its top she turned slowly, trying to find some
proof that she had not been tossed alone into this
strange world.

Save for the figures of stone and beds of rank-
looking growth there was nothing to be seen.
The wall and the dome lay below. But behind her
when she faced the dome was a second slope
leading to a still higher point which was
crowned by a roof to be seen only in bits and
patches through a screen of oarn trees. The roof
had a ridge which terminated at either side in a
sharp upcurve, giving the building the odd appearance of having an ear on either end. It was
green with a glittering surface, almost brilliantly
so in spite of the clouds overhead.

To her right and left Tamisan caught glimpses
of the wall curving and of more stone figures and
flower or shrub plantings. Gathering up her
skirts more firmly, she began to walk up the
curve of the higher slope in search of some road
or path leading to the roof.

She came across what she sought as she de-
toured to avoid a thicket of heavy brush in which
were impaled huge scarlet flowers. It was a wide
roadway paved with small colored pebbles em-
bedded in a solid surface, and it led from an open

gateway up the swell of the slope to the front of the structure.

In shape the building was vaguely familiar, though Tamisan could not identify it. Perhaps it resembled something she had seen in the tri-dees. The door was of the same brilliant green as the roof, but the walls were a pale yellow, cut sharply at regular intervals by very narrow windows, so tall that they ran from floor to roof level.

Even as she stood there wondering where she had seen such a house before, a woman came out. As did Tamisan, she wore a long skirted robe with laced bodice and slit sleeves. But her's was the same green as that of the door, so that, standing against it, only her head and arms were clearly visible. She gestured with vigor, and Tamisan suddenly realized that it must be she who was being summoned as if she were expected.

Again she fought down unease. In dreams she was well used to meetings and partings, but always those were of her own devising and did not happen for a purpose which was not of her wish. Her dream people were toys, game pieces, to be moved hither and thither at her will, she being always in command of them.

"Tamisan, they wait; come quickly!" the woman called.

Tamisan was minded in that instant to run in the other direction, but the need to learn what had happened made her take what might be the dangerous course of joining the woman.

"Fha, you are wet! This is no hour for walking in the garden. The First Standing asks for a read-

ing from the Mouth. If you would have lavishly
from her purse, hurry, lest she grows too impa-
tient to wait!''

The door gave upon a narrow entry and the
woman in green propelled Tamisan towards a
second opening directly facing her. She came
into the large room where a circle of couches was
centered. By each stood a small table now burdened with dishes which serving maids were
bearing away as if a meal had just been concluded. Tall candlesticks, matching Tamisan's
own height, stood also between the divans; the
candles in each, as thick as her forearm, were
alight, to give forth not only radiance but also a
sweet odor as they burned.

Midpoint in the divan circle was a tall-backed
chair over which arched a canopy. In it sat a
woman, a goblet in her hand. She had a fur cloak
pulled about her shoulders hiding almost all of
her robe, save that here and there a shimmer of
gold caught fire from the candlelight. Only her
face was visible in a hood of the same metal-like
fabric, and it was that of a very old woman,
seamed with deep wrinkles, sunken of eye.

The divans, Tamisan marked, were occupied
by both men and women, the women flanking
the chair and the men farthest away from the
ancient noblewoman. Directly facing her was a
second impressive chair, lacking only the
canopy; before it was a table on which stood, at
each of its four corners, small basins: one cream,
one pale rose, one faintly blue, and the fourth
sea-foam green.

Tamisan's store of knowledge gave her some

preparation. This was the setting for the magic of
a Mouth, and it was apparent that her services as
a foreseer were about to be demanded. What had
she done in allowing herself to be drawn here?
Could she make pretense her savant well enough
to deceive this company?

"I hunger, Mouth of Olava; I hunger not for
that which will feed the body, but for that which
satisfies the mind." The old woman leaned forward a little. Her voice might be the thin one of
age, but it carried with it the force of authority, of
one who has not had her word or desire questioned for a long time.

She must improvise, Tamisan knew. She was a
dreamer and she had wrought in dreams many
strange things, let her but remember that. Her
damp skirts clung clammily to her legs and
thighs as she came forward, saying nothing to
the woman in return, but seating herself in the
chair facing her client. She was drawing on
faint stirrings of a memory which seemed not
truly her own for guidance, though she had not
yet realized that fully.

"What would you know, First Standing?" She
raised her hands to her forehead in an instinctive
gesture, touching forefingers to her temples,
right and left.

"What comes to me . . . and mine." The last
two words had come almost as an afterthought.

Tamisan's hands went out without her conscious ordering. She stifled her amazement. It
was as if she were repeating an act as well
learned as her dreamer's technique had been.
With her left hand she gathered up a palmful of

the sand from the cream bowl. It was a shade or two darker than the container. She tossed this with a sharp movement of her wrist and it settled smoothly as a film on the table top.

What she was doing was not of her conscious mind, as if another had taken charge of her actions. By the way the woman in the chair leaned forward, and by the hush which had fallen on her companion, this was right and proper.

Without any order from her mind, Tamisan's right hand went now to the blue bowl with its dark blue sand. But this was not tossed. Instead, she held the fine grains in her upright fist, passing it slowly over the table top so that a very tiny trickle of grit fed down to make a pattern on the first film.

It was a pattern, not a random scattering. What she had so drawn was a recognizable sword with a basket shaped hilt and a slightly curved blade tapering to a narrow point.

Now her hand moved to the pink bowl. The sand she gathered up there was a dark red, more vivid than the other colors, as if she dealt now with flecks of newly shed blood. Once more she used her upheld fist, and the shifting stream fed from her palm became a space ship! It was slightly different in outline from those she had seen all her life, but it was unmistakably a ship, and it was drawn on the table top as if it threatened to descend upon the pointed sword. *Or is it that the sword threatens it?*

She heard a gasp of surprise, or was it fear? But that sound had not come from the woman who had bade her foretell. It must have broken from

some other member of the company intent upon
Tamisan's painting with the flowing sand.

It was to the fourth bowl now that her right
hand moved. But she did not take up a full fist-
ful, rather a generous pinch between thumb and
forefinger. She held the sand high above the
picture and released it. The green specks floated
down—to gather in a sign like a circle with one
portion missing.

She stared at that and it seemed to alter a little
under the intensity of her gaze. What it had
changed to was a symbol she knew well, one
which brought a small gasp from her. It was the
seal, simplified it was true, but still readable, of
the House of Starrex, and it overlaid both the
edge of the ship and the tip of the sword.

"Read you this!" the noblewoman demanded
sharply.

From somewhere the words came readily to
Tamisan. "The sword is the sword of Ty-Kry
raised in defense."

"Assured, assured." A murmur ran along the
divans.

"The ship comes as a danger."

"That thing—a ship? But it is no ship."

"It is a ship from the stars."

"And woe—woe and woe—" That was no
murmur, but a full-throated cry of fright. "As in
the days of our fathers when we had to deal with
the false ones. Ahtap—let the spirit of Ahta be
shield to our arms, a sword in our hands!"

The noblewoman made a silencing gesture
with one hand. "Enough! Crying to the revered
spirits may bring sustenance, but they are not

noted for helping those not standing to arms on their own behalf. There have been other sky ships since Ahta's days, and with them we have dealt—to our purpose. If another comes we are forewarned, which is also forearmed. But what lies there in green, oh, Mouth of Olava, which surprised even you?"

Tamisan had had precious moments in which to think. If it were true, as she had deduced, that she was tied to this world by those she had brought with her, then she must find them; and it was clear that they were not of this company. Therefore, this last must be made to work for her.

"The green sign is that of a champion, one meant to be mighty in the coming battle. But he shall not be known save when the sign points to him, and it may be that this can only be seen by one with the gift."

She looked to the noblewoman, and, meeting those old eyes, Tamisan felt a small chill rise in her, one which had not been born from the still damp clothing she wore. There was that in those two shadowed eyes which questioned coldly and did not accept without proof.

"So should the one with the gift you speak of go sniffing all through Ty-Kry and the land beyond the city, even to the boundaries of the world?"

"If need be." Tamisan stood firm.

"A long journey mayhap, and many strides into danger. And if the ship comes before this champion is found? A thin cord I think oh, Mouth, on which to hang the future of a city, a kingdom, or a people. Look if you will but I say we have more tested ways of dealing with these interlopers from the skies. But, Mouth, since you have given warning, let it so be remembered."

She put her hands on the arms of her chair and arose, using them to lever her. So did all her company come to their feet, two of the women hurrying to her so that she could lay her hands upon their shoulders for support. Without another look at Tamisan she went, nor did the dreamer rise to see her go. For suddenly she was spent, tired as she had been in the past when a dream broke and left her supine and drained. But this dream did not break; it kept her sitting before the table and its sand pictures, looking at that green symbol, still caught fast in the web of another world.

The woman in green returned, bearing a goblet in her two hands and offering it to Tamisan.

"The First Standing will go to the High Castle and the Over-queen. She turned into that road. Drink, Tamisan, and mayhap the Over-queen herself will ask you for a seeing."

Tamisan? That was her true name; twice this woman had called her by it. *How is it known in a dream?* Yet she dared not to ask that question or any of the others she needed answer to. Instead she drank from the goblet, finding the hot, spicy liquid driving the chill from her body.

There was so much she must learn and must know; but she could not discover it, save indirectly, lest she reveal what she was and was not.

"I am tired."

"There is a resting place prepared," the woman returned. "You have only to come."

Tamisan had almost to lever herself up as the noblewoman had done. She was giddy and had to catch at the back of the chair. Then she moved after her hostess, hoping desperately to know.

III

Did one sleep in a dream, dream upon dream, perhaps? Tamisan wondered as she stretched out upon the couch her hostess showed her. Yet when she set aside her crown, laid her head upon the roll which served as a pillow, she was once more alert, her thoughts racing, or entangled in such wild confusion that she felt as giddy as she had upon rising from her seer's chair.

The Starrex symbol overlying both that of the sword and the space ship in the sand picture, could it mean that she would only find what she sought when the might of this world met that of the starmen? Had she indeed in some manner fallen into the past where she would relive the first coming of the space voyagers to Ty-Kry? But the noblewoman had mentioned past encounters with them which had ended in favor of Ty-Kry.

Tamisan had tried to envision a world of her own time, but one in which history had taken a different road. Yet much of that around her was of the past. Did that mean that, without the decisions of her own time, the world of Ty-Kry remained largely unchanged from century to century?

Real, unreal, old, new. She had lost all a

dreamer's command of action. Tamisan did not play now with toys which she could move about at will, but rather was caught up in a series of events she could not foresee and over which she had no control. Yet twice the woman had called her by her rightful name and, without willing it, she had used the devices of a Mouth of Olava to foretell, as if she had done so many times before.

Could it be? Tamisan closed her teeth upon her lower lip and felt the pain of that, just as she felt the pain of the bruises left by her abrupt entrance into the mysterious here. *Could it be that some dreams are so deep, so well woven, that they are to the dreamer real? Is this indeed the fate of those "closed" dreamers who were worthless for the Hive? Do they in their trances live a countless number of lives?* But she was not a closed dreamer.

Awake! Once more, stretched as she was upon the couch, she used the proper technique to throw herself out of a dream, and once more she experienced that weird nothingness in which she spun sickeningly, as if held helplessly in some void, tied to an anchor which held her back from the full leap to sane safety. There was only one explanation, that somewhere in this strange Ty-Kry one or both of those who had prepared to share her dream was now to be found and must be sought out before she could return.

So—the sooner that is accomplished, the better! But where should I start seeking? Though a feeling of weakness clung to her limbs, making her move slowly as if she strove to walk against the pull of a strong current, Tamisan arose from the couch. She turned to pick up her Mouth's crown, and so looked into the oval of a mirror, startled thus into immobility. For the figure she looked upon as her own reflection was not that she had seen before.

It was not the robe and the crown which had changed her; she was not the same person. For a long time, ever since she could remember, she had had the pallid skin, the close cropped hair of a dreamer very seldom in the sunlight. But the face of the woman in the mirror was a soft, even brown. The cheekbones were wide, the eyes large and the lips very red. Her brows—she leaned closer to the mirror to see what gave them that odd upward slant and decided that they had been plucked or shaven to produce the effect. Her hair was perhaps three fingers long and not the well known fair coloring, but dark and curling. She was not the Tamisan she knew, nor was this stranger the product of her own will.

It would follow logically that if she did not look like her normal self, then perhaps the two she sought were no longer as she remembered either. Thus her search would be twice as difficult. Could she ever recognize them?

Frightened, she sat down on the couch facing the mirror. She dared not give way to fear, for if she once let it break her control she might be utterly lost. Logic, even in such a world of unlogic, must make her think lucidly.

Just how true was her soothsaying? At least she had not influenced that fall of the sand. Perhaps the Mouth of Olava did have supernatural powers. She had played with the idea of magic in the past to embroider dreams, but that had been her own creation. Could she use it by will now? It would seem this unknown self of hers did manage to draw upon some unknown source of power.

She must fasten her thoughts upon one of the men and hold him in her mind. Could the dream tie pull her to Kas or Starrex? All she knew of her master she had learned from tapes, and tapes gave one only superficial knowledge. One could not well study a person going through only half-understood actions behind a veil which concealed more than it displayed. Kas had spoken directly to her, his flesh had touched hers. If she must choose one to draw her, then it had better be Kas.

In her mind Tamisan built a memory picture of him as she would build a preliminary picture for a dream. Then suddenly the Kas in her mind flickered, changed; she saw another man. He was taller than the Kas she knew, and he wore a uniform tunic and space boots; his features were hard to distinguish. That vision lasted only a fraction of time.

The ship! The symbol had lain touching both ship and sword in the sand seeing. It would be easier to seek a man on a ship than wandering through the streets of a strange city with no better clue than that Starrex's counterpart might be there.

It was so little on which to pin a quest: a ship which might or might not be now approaching Ty-Kry, and which would meet a drastic reception when it landed. *Suppose Kas, or his double, is killed? Would that anchor me here for all* time? Resolutely Tamisan pushed such negative speculation to the back of her mind. *First things first; the ship has not yet planeted.* But when it came she must make sure that she was among those preparing for its welcome.

It seemed that having made that decision she was at last able to sleep, for the fatigue which had struck at her in the hall returned a hundred fold and she fell back on the couch as one drugged, remembering nothing more until she awakened. She found the woman in green standing above her, one hand on her shoulder shaking her gently back to awareness.

"Awake, there is a summons."

A summons to dream, Tamisan thought dazedly, and then the unfamiliar room and the immediate past came completely back to her.

"The First Standing Jassa has summoned." The woman sounded excited. "It is said by her messenger—he has brought a chair cart for you—that you are to go to the High Castle! Perhaps you will see for the Over-queen herself! But there is time—I have won it for you—to bathe, to eat, to change your robe. See, I have plundered my own bride chest." She pointed to a chair over which was spread a robe, not of the deep violet Tamisan now wore, but of a purple-wine. "It is the only one of the proper color—or near it." She ran her hand lovingly over the rich folds.

"But haste," she added briskly. "As a Mouth you can claim the need for making ready to appear before high company, but to linger too long will raise the anger of the First Standing."

There was a basin large enough to serve as a

bath in the room beyond, and, as well as the robe, the woman had brought fresh body linen. When Tamisan stood once more before the mirror to clasp her silver belt and assume the Mouth crown, she felt renewed and refreshed and her thanks were warm.

But the woman made a gesture of brushing them aside. "Are we not of the same clan, cousin? Shall one say that Nahra is not open-handed with her own? That you are a Mouth is our clan pride, let us enjoy it through you!"

She brought a covered bowl and a goblet and Tamisan ate a dish of meal into which had been baked dried fruit and bits of what she thought well chopped meat. It was tasty and she finished it to the last crumb, just as she emptied the cup of a tart-sweet drink.

"Wellaway, Tamisan, this is a great day for the clan of Fremont, when you go to the High Castle and perhaps stand before the Over-queen. May it be that the seeing is not for ill, but for good. Though you are but the Mouth of Olava and not the One dealing fortune to us who live and die."

"For your aid and your good wishing, receive my thanks," Tamisan said. "I, too, hope that fortune comes before misfortune on this day." And that is stark truth, she thought, for I must gather fortune to me with both hands and hold it tight, lest the game I play be lost.

First Standing Jassa's messenger was an officer, his hair clubbed up under a ridged helm to give additional protection to his head in battle, his breastplate, enameled blue with the double crown of the Over-queen, and his sword very much to the fore. It was as if he already

strode the street of a city at war. There was a
small griffin between the shafts of the chair cart
and two men at arms ready, one at the griffin's
head, the other holding aside the curtains as
their officer handed Tamisan into the chair. He
briskly jerked the curtains shut without asking
her pleasure, and she decided that perhaps her
visit to the High Castle was to be a secret matter.

Between the curtain edges she caught sight of
this Ty-Kry, and, though in parts it was very
strange to her, there were enough similarities to
provide her with an anchor to the real. The sky
towers and other off-world forms of architecture
which had been introduced by space travelers
were missing. But the streets themselves and
the many beds of foliage and flowers were those
she had known all her life.

The High Castle—she drew a deep breath as
they wound out of town and along the river—
had been part of her world, too, though then as a
ruined and very ancient landmark. Part of it had
been consumed in the war of Sylt's rebellion,
and it had been considered a place of misfortune,
largely shunned, save for off-world tourists seeking the unusual.

Here it was in its pride, larger and more widely
spread then in her Ty-Kry, as if the generations
who had deserted it in her world had clung to it
here, adding ever to its bulk. It was not a single
structure, but a city in itself. However, it had no
merchants or public buildings. It provided
homes to shelter the nobles who must spend part
of the year at court, all their servants and the
many officials of the kingdom.

In its heart was the building which gave it its

name, a collection of towers, rising far above the
lesser structures at the foot. The buildings' walls
were gray at their bases and changed subtly as
they arose until their tops were a deep, rich blue.
The other buildings in the great pile were wholly
gray as to wall, a darker blue as to roof.

The chair creaked forward on its two wheels,
the griffin being kept to a steady pace by the man
at its head, and passed under the thick arch in
the outer wall, then up a street between buildings which, though dwarfed by the towers, were
in turn dwarfing to those who walked or rode by
them.

There was a second gate, more buildings, a
third gate and then the open space about the
central towers. They passed people in plenty
since they had entered the first gate. Many were
soldiers of the guard, but some of the armed men
had worn other colors and insignia, being,
Tamisan guessed, the retainers of court lords.
Now and then some lord came proudly, his ret-
inue strung along behind him by threes to make
a show which amused Tamisan. *As if the
number of followers to tread on one's heels en-
hanced one's importance in the world.*

She was handed down with a little more ceremony than she had been ushered into the chair,
and the officer offered her his wrist, his men
falling in behind as a groom hurried forward to
lead off the equipage, thus affording her a tail of
honor, too.

But the towers of the High Castle were so awe-
inspiring, so huge a pile, that she was glad she
had an escort into their heart. The farther they

advanced through the halls, the more uneasy she became. It was as if once she were within this maze there might be no retreat and she would be lost forever.

Twice they climbed staircases until her legs ached with the effort and they took on the aspect of mountains. Then her party passed into a long hall which was lighted not only by the candle trees, but by thin rays filtering through windows placed so high above their heads that nothing could be seen through them. Tamisan, in that part of her which seemed familiar with this world, knew this to be the Walk of the Nobles, and the company now gathered here were the Third Standing, nearest, then the Second, and, at the far end of that road of blue carpet onto which her guide led her, First Standing. They were sitting; there were two arcs of hooded and canopied chairs, with above them a throne on a three-step dias. The hood over that was upheld by a double crown which glittered with gems. On the steps were grouped men in the armor of the guard and others wearing bright tunics, their hair loose upon their shoulders.

It was toward that throne that the officer led her and they passed through the ranks of the Third Standing, hearing a low murmur of voices. Tamisan looked neither to right nor left; she wished to see the Over-queen, for it was plain she was being granted full audience. Something stirred deep within her as if a small pin pricked. The reason for this she did not know, save that ahead was something of vast importance to her.

Now they were equal with the first of the

chairs and she saw that the greater number of those who so sat were women, but not all. Mainly they were at least in middle life. So Tamisan came to the foot of the dias, and in that moment she did not go to one knee as did the officer, but rather raised her finger tips to touch the rim of the crown on her head; for with another of those flashes of half recognition she knew that in this place that which she represented did not bow as did others, but acknowledged only that the Queen was one to whom human allegiance was granted after another and greater loyalty was paid elsewhere.

The Over-queen looked down with a deeply searching stare as Tamisan looked up. What Tamisan saw was a woman to whom she could not set an age; she might be either old or young, for the years had not seemed to mark her. The robe on her full figure was not ornate, but a soft pearl color without ornamentation, save that she wore a girdle of silvery chains braided and woven together, and a collarlike necklace of the same metal from which fringed milky gems cut into drops. Her hair was a flame of brightly-glowing red, in which a diadem of the same creamy stones was almost hidden. Was she beautiful? Tamisan could not have said; but that she was vitally alive there was no doubt. Even though she sat quietly there was an aura of energy about her suggesting that this was only a pause between the doing of great and necessary deeds. She was the most assertive personality Tamisan had ever seen, and instantly the guards of a dreamer went into action. To serve such a

mistress, Tamisan thought, would sap all the
personality from one, so that the servant would
become but a mirror to reflect from that moment
of surrender onward.

"Welcome, Mouth of Olava who has been ut-
tering strange things." The Over-queen's voice
was mocking, challenging.

"A Mouth says naught, Great One, save what
is given it to speak." Tamisan found her answer
ready, though she had not consciously formed it
in her mind.

"So we were told, though gods may grow old
and tired. Or is that only the fate of men? But
now, it is our will that Olava speak again if that is
fortune for this hour. So be it!"

As if that last phrase were an order, there was a
stir among those standing on the steps of the
throne. Two of the guards brought out a table, a
third a stool, the fourth a tray on which rested
four bowls of sand. These they set up before the
throne.

Tamisan took her place on the stool, again put
her finger to her temples. Would this work again,
or must she try to force a picture in the sand? She
felt a small shiver of nerves she fought to control.

"What desires the Great One?" She was glad to
hear her voice steady, no hint of her uneasiness
in it.

"What chances in, say, four passages of the
sun?"

Tamisan waited. Would that other personality, or power, or whatever it might be, take over?
Her hand did not move. Instead, that odd, disturbing prick grew the stronger; she was drawn,

even as a noose might be laid about her forehead
to pull her head around. So she turned to follow
the dictates of that pull and looked where something willed her eyes to look. All she saw was the
line of officers on the steps of the throne, and
they stared at and through her, none with any
sign of recognition. *Starrex!* She grasped at that
hope, but none of them resembled the man she
sought.

"Does Olava sleep? Or had His Mouth been
forgotten for a space?"

The Over-queen's voice was sharper and
Tamisan broke that hold on her attention, looking back to the throne and the woman on it.

"It is not meet for the Mouth to speak unless
Olava wishes." Tamisan began, feeling increas-
ingly nervous. That sensation gripped her left
hand, as if it were not under her control but
possessed by another will. She fell silent as it
gathered up the brownish sand and tossed it to
form a picture's background.

This time she did not seek next the blue grains;
rather her fist dug into the red and moved to
paint the outline of the space ship, above it a
single red circle.

Then, there was a moment of hesitation before
her fingers strayed to the green, took up a generous pinch and again made Starrex's symbol
below the ship.

"A single sun," the Over-queen read out. "One
day until the enemy comes. But what is the re-
maining word of Olava, Mouth?"

"That there be one among you who is a key
to victory. He shall stand against the enemy
and under him fortune comes."

"So? Who is this hero?"

Tamisan looked again to the line of officers. Dared she trust to instinct? Something within her urged her on.

"Let each of these protectors of Ty-Kry"—she raised a finger to indicate the officers—"come forward and take up the sand of seeing. Let the Mouth touch that hand and may it then strew the answer. Perhaps Olava will make it clear in this manner."

To Tamisan's surprise the Over-queen laughed. "As good a way as any perhaps for picking a champion. To abide by Olava's choice, that is another matter." Her smile faded as she glanced at the men, as if there was a thought in her mind which disturbed her.

At her nod they came one by one. Under the shadows of their helmets their faces, being of one race, were very similar and Tamisan, studying each, could see no chance of telling which Starrex might be.

Each took up a pinch of green sand, held out his hand, palm down, and let the grains fall while she set finger tip to his knuckles. The sand drifted but in no shape and to no purpose.

It was not until the last man came that there was a difference, for then the sand did not drift, but fell to form again the symbol which was twin to the one already on the table. Tamisan looked up. The officer was staring at the sand rather than meeting her eyes, and there was a line of strain about his mouth, a look about him as might shadow the face of a man who stood with his back to a wall and a ring of sword points at his throat.

"This is your man," Tamisan said. Starrex? She must be sure; if she could only demand the truth in this instant!

But her preoccupation was swept aside.

"Olava deals falsely!" That cry came from the officer behind her, the one who had brought her here.

"Perhaps we must not think ill of Olava's advice." The Over-queen's voice had a guttural, feline purr. "It may be his Mouth is not wholly wedded to his service, but speaks for others than Olava at times. Hawarel, so you are to be our champion?"

The officer went to one knee, his hands clasped loosely before him as if he wished all to see he did not reach for any weapon.

"I am no choice, save the Great One's." In spite of the strain visible in his tense body he spoke levelly and without a tremor.

"Great One, this traitor—" Two of the officers moved as if to lay hands upon him and drag him away.

"No. Has not Olava spoken?" The mockery was very plain in the Over-queen's tone now. "But to make sure that Olava's will be carried out, take good care of our champion-to-be. Since Hawarel is to fight our battle with the cursed starmen, he must be saved to do it. And,"—now she looked to Tamisan, startled by the quick turn of events and their hostility to Olava's choice— "let the Mouth of Olava share with Hawarel this waiting that she may, perhaps, instill in Olava's choice the vigor and strength such a battle will demand of our chosen champion." Each time the

Over-queen spoke the word "champion" she
made of it a thing of derision and subtle menace.

"The audience is finished." The Over-queen
arose and stepped behind the throne as those
about Tamisan fell to their knees; then she was
gone. But the officer who had guided Tamisan
was by her side. Hawarel, once more on his feet,
was closely flanked by two of the other guards,
one of whom pulled their prisoner's sword from
his sheath before he could move. Then, with
Hawarel before her, Tamisan was urged from the
hall, though none laid a hand on her.

At the moment she was pleased enough to go,
hoping for a chance to prove the rightness of her
guess, that Hawarel and Starrex were the same
and she had found the first of her fellow dreamers.

They transversed more halls until they came
to a door which one of Hawarel's guards opened.
The prisoner walked through and Tamisan's escort waved her after him. Then the door slammed shut, and at that sound Hawarel whirled
around.

Under the beaking foreplate of his helmet his
eyes were cold fire and he seemed a man about to
leap for his enemy's throat.

His voice was only a harsh whisper. "Who—
who set you to my death wishing, witch?"

IV

His hands reached for her throat. Tamisan
flung up her arm in an attempt to guard and
stumbled back.

"Lord Starrex!" *If I have been wrong—if . . .*

Though his finger tips brushed her shoulders, he did not grasp her. Instead it was his turn to retreat a step or two, his mouth half open in a gasp.

"Witch! Witch!" The very force of the words he hurled at her made them darts dispatched from one of the crossbows of the history tapes.

"Lord Starrex," Tamisan repeated, feeling on more secure ground at his stricken amazement and no longer fearing he would attack her out of hand. His reaction to that name was enough to assure her she was right, though he did not seem prepared to acknowledge it.

"I am Hawarel of the Vanora." He brought out those words as harsh croaking.

Tamisan glanced around. This was a bare-walled room, with no hiding place for a listener. In her own time and place she could have feared many scanning devices, but she thought those unknown to this Ty-Kry. To win Hawarel-Starrex into cooperation was very necessary.

"You are Lord Starrex," she returned with bold confidence, or at least what she hoped was a convincing show of it. Just as I am Tamisan, the dreamer. And this, wherein we are caught, is the dream you ordered of me."

He raised his hand to his forehead, his fingers encountered his helmet and he swept it off unheedingly, so that it clanked and skid across the polished floor. His hair, netted into a kind of protecting cushion was piled about his head, giving him an odd appearance to Tamisan. It was black and thick, just as his skin was as brown-hued as that of her new body. Without the shadow of the helm, she could see his face more clearly, finding in it no resemblance to the aloof master of the sky towers. In a way, it was that of a younger man, one less certain of himself.

"I am Hawarel," he repeated doggedly. "You try to trap me, or perhaps the trap has already closed and you seek now to make me condemn myself with my own mouth. I tell you, I am no traitor. I am Hawarel and my blood oath to the Great One has been faithfully kept."

Tamisan experienced a rise of impatience. She had not thought Lord Starrex to be a stupid man. But it would seem his counterpart here lacked more than just the face of his other self.

"You are Starrex, and this is a dream!" If it was not she did not care to raise that issue now. "Remember the sky tower? You bought me from Jabis for dreaming. Then you summoned me and Lord Kas and ordered me to prove my worth."

His brows drew together in a black frown as he stared at her.

"What have they given you, or promised, that you do this to me?" came his counterdemand. "I am no sworn enemy to you or yours—not that I know."

Tamisan sighed. "Do you deny you know the name Starrex?" she asked.

For a long moment he was silent. Then he turned from her, took a stride or two; his toe thumped against his helmet, sending it rolling ahead of him. She waited. He turned again to face her.

"You are a Mouth of Olava. . . ."

She shook her head, interrupting him. "We have little time for such fencing, Lord Starrex. You do know that name, and it is in my mind that you also remember the rest, at least in some measure. I am Tamisan the dreamer."

It was his turn to sigh. "So you say."

"So I shall continue to say, and, mayhap as I do, others than you will listen."

"As I thought!" he flashed. "You would have me betray myself."

"If you are truly Hawarel as you state, then what have you to betray?"

"Very well. I am—am two! I am Hawarel and I am someone else who has queer memories and who may well be a night demon come to dispute ownership of this body. There, you have it. Go and tell those who sent you and have me out to the arrow range for a quick ending there. Perhaps that will be better than to continue as a battlefield between two different selves."

Perhaps he was not just being obstinate, Tamisan thought. It might be that the dream had a greater hold on him than it did on her. After all, she was a trained dreamer, one used to venturing into illusions wrought from imagination.

"If you can remember a little, then listen." She drew closer to him and began to speak in a lower voice, not that she believed they could be overheard, but it was well to take no chance. Swiftly she gave her account of the whole tangle, or what had been her part in it.

When she was done she was surprised to see that a certain hardening had overtaken his features, so that now he looked more resolute, less like one trapped in a maze which had no guide.

"And this is the truth?"

"By what god or power do you wish me to swear to it?" She was exasperated now, frustrated by his lingering doubts.

"None, because it explains what was heretofore unexplainable—what has made my life a hell of doubt these past hours, and brought more suspicion upon me. I have been two persons. But if this is all a dream, why is that so?"

"I do not know." Tamisan chose frankness as best befitting her needs. "This is unlike any dream I have created before."

"In what manner?" he asked crisply.

"It is a part of a dreamer's duty to study her master's personality, to suit his desires, even if those be unexpressed and hidden. From what I had learned of you, of Lord Starrex, I thought that too much had been already seen, experienced and known to you—that it must be a new approach I tried, or else you would find that dreaming held no profit.

"Therefore it came to me suddenly that I would not dream of the past, nor of the future, which are the common approaches for an action dreamer, but refine upon the subject. In the past there were times in history when the future rested upon a single decision. And it was in my mind to select certain of these decisions and then envision a world in which those decisions had gone in the opposite direction—trying to see what would be the present result of actions in the past."

"So this is what you tried? And what decisions did you select for your experiment at the
rewriting of history?" He was giving her his full
attention.

"I took three. First, the welcome of the Over-
queen Ahta, second, the drift of the colony ship
Wanderer, third, the rebellion of Sylt. Should
the welcome have been a rejection, should the
colony ship never reach here, should Sylt have
failed—these would produce a world I thought
might be interesting to visit in a dream. So I read
what history tapes I could call upon. Thus, when
you summoned me to dream I had my ideas
ready. But it did not work as it should have.
Instead of spinning the proper dream, creating
incidents in good order, I found myself fast
caught in a world I did not know or build."

As she spoke she could watch the change in
him. He had lost all the fervent antagonism of his
first attack on her. More and more she could see
what she had associated with the personality of
Lord Starrex coming through the unfamiliar envelope of this man's body.

"So it did not work properly."

"No. As I have said, I found myself in the
dream, with no control of action and no recognizable creation factors. I do not understand—"

"No? There could be an explanation." The
frown line was back between his brows, but it
was not a scowl aimed at her. It was as if he were
trying hard to remember something of importance which eluded his efforts. "There is a
theory, a very old one. Yes, that of parallel
worlds."

In her wide use of the tapes she had not come

across that, and now she demanded the knowledge of him almost fiercely. "What are those?"

"You are not the first, how could you be, to be struck by the notion that sometimes history and the future hang upon a very thin cord which can be twisted this way and that by a small chance. A theory was once advanced that when that chanced it created a second world, one in which the decision was made to the right, when that of the world we know went to the left."

"But alternate worlds—where—how did they exist?"

"Thus, perhaps"—he held out his two hands horizontally, one above the other—"in layers. There were even old tales created for amusement, of men traveling not back in time, nor forward, but across it from one such world to another."

"But here we are. I am a Mouth of Olava and I don't look like myself, just as to the eye you are not Lord Starrex."

"Perhaps we are the people we would be if our world had taken the other side of your three decisions. It is a clever device for a dreamer to create, Tamisan—"

She told him now the last truth. "Only, I do not think I have created it. Certainly I cannot control it—"

"You have tried to break this dream?"

"Of course, but I am tied here. Perhaps it is by you, and Lord Kas. Until we three try together maybe we cannot any of us return."

"Now you must go searching for him with that board and sand trick of yours?"

She shook her head. "Kas, I think, is one of the

crew on the spacer about to set down. I believe I saw him—though not his face." She smiled a little shakily. "It seems that though I am mainly the Tamisan I have always been, yet also do I have some of the powers of a Mouth; likewise, you are Hawarel as well as Starrex."

"The longer I listen to you," he announced, "the more I become Starrex. So we must find Kas on the spacer before we wriggle free from this tangle? But that is going to be rather a problem. I am enough of Hawarel to know that the spacer is going to receive the usual welcome dealt off-world ships here: trickery and extinction. Your three points have been as you envisioned them. There was no welcome, but rather a massacre; no colony ship ever reached here, and Sylt was speared by a contemptuous man at arms the first time he lifted his voice to draw a crowd. Hawarel knows this as truth; as Starrex I am aware there is another truth which did radically change life on this planet. Now, did you seek me out on purpose, your champion tale intended to be our bridge to Kas?"

"No, at least I did not consciously arrange it so. I tell you, I have some of the power of a Mouth—they take over."

He gave a sharp bark of sound which was not laughter but somewhat akin to it. "By the fist of Jimsam Taragon, we have it complicated by magic, too! And I suppose you cannot tell me just how much a Mouth can do in the way of foreseeing, forearming or freeing us from this trap?"

Tamisan shook her head. "The Mouths were

mentioned in the history tapes; they were very
important once. But after Sylt's rebellion they
were either killed or disappeared. They were
hunted by both sides, and most we know about
them is only legend. I cannot tell you what I can
do. Sometimes something, perhaps the memory
and knowledge of this body, takes over and then
I do strange things. I neither will nor understand
them."

He crossed the room and pulled two stools
from a far corner. "We might as well sit at ease
and explore what we can of this world's
memories. It just might be that united, we can
learn more than when trying alone. The trouble
is—" He reached out a hand and mechanically
she touched finger tips to the back of it in an
oddly formal ceremony which was not part of
her own knowledge. He guided her to one of the
stools and she was glad to sit down.

"The trouble is," he repeated as he dropped on
the other stool, stretching out his long legs and
tugging at his sword belt with that dangerously
empty sheath, "that I was more than a little
mixed up when I awoke, if you might call it that,
in this body. My first reactions must have
suggested mental imbalance to those I encountered. Luckily, the Hawarel part was in control
soon enough to save me. But there is a second
drawback to this identity: I am suspect as coming from a province where there has been a rebellion. In fact, I am here in Ty-Kry as a hostage,
rather than a member of the guard in good standing. I have not been able to ask questions, and all
I have learned is in bits and pieces. The real

Hawarel is a quite uncomplicated, simple sol-
dier who is hurt by the suspicion against him
and quite fervently loyal to the crown. I wonder
how Kas took his waking. If he preserves any
remnant of his real self he ought to be well established by now."

Surprised, Tamisan asked a question to which
she hoped he would give a true and open answer. "You do not like—you have reason to fear
Lord Kas?"

"Like? Fear?" She could see that thin shadow
of Starrex overlaying Hawarel become more distinct. "Those are emotions. I have had little to do
with emotions for some time."

"But you wanted him to share the dream," she
persisted.

"True. I may not be emotional about my es-
teemed cousin, but I am a prudent man. Since it
was by his urging, in fact his arrangement, that
you were added to my household, I thought it
only fair he share in his plan for my entertain-
ment. I know that Kas is very solicitous of his
crippled cousin, ready handed to serve in any
way, so generous of his time and his energy—"

"You suspect him of something?" She
thought she had sensed what lay behind his
words.

"Suspect? Of what? He has been, as all would
assure you freely, my good friend, as far as I
would allow." There was a closed look about
him warning her off any further exploration of
that.

"His crippled cousin." This time Hawarel repeated those words as if he spoke to himself and

not to her. "At least you have done me a small service on the credit side of the scale." Now he did look to Tamisan as he thumped his right leg with a satisfaction which was not of the Starrex she knew. "You have provided me with a body in good working order, which I may well need since, so far, bad has outweighed the good in this world."

"Hawarel, Lord Starrex—" She was beginning when he interrupted her.

"Give me always Hawarel, remember. There is no need to add to the already heavy load of suspicion surrounding me in these halls."

"Hawarel, then, I did not choose you for the champion; that was done by a power I do not understand, working through me. If they agree, you have a good chance to find Kas. You may even demand that he be the one you battle."

"Find him how?"

"They may allow me to select the proper one from the off-world force," she suggested. It was a very thin thread on which to hang any plan of escape, but she could not see a better one.

"And you think that this sand painting will pick him out, as it did me?"

"It did you, did it not?"

"That I cannot deny."

"And the first time I foresaw, for one of the First Standing, it made such an impression on her that she had me summoned here to foresee for the Over-queen."

"Magic!" Again he uttered that half laugh.

"To another world much that the space travelers can do might be termed magic."

"Well said. I have seen strange things—yes, I have seen things myself, and not while dreaming either. Very well, I am to volunteer to meet an enemy champion from the ship and then you sand paint out the proper one. If you are successful and do find Kas, then what?"

"It is simple; we wake."

"You take us with you, of course?"

"If we are so linked that we cannot leave here without one another, then a single waking will take us all."

"Are you sure you need Kas? After all, I was the one you were planning this dream for."

"We go, leave Lord Kas here?"

"A cowardly withdrawal you think, my dreamer. But one, I assure you, which would solve many things. However, can you send me through and return for Kas? It is in my mind I would like to know what is happening now for myself in our own world. Is it not by the dreamer's oath that he for whom the dream is wrought has first call upon the dreamer?"

He did have some lurking uneasiness tied to Kas, but in a manner he was right. She reached out before he was aware of what she would do and seized his hand, at the same time using the formula for waking. Once more that mist which was nowhere enveloped her. But it was no use, her first guess had been right, they were still tied. She blinked her eyes open upon the same room. Hawarel had slumped and was falling from his stool, so that she had to go to one knee to support his body with her shoulder or he would have slid full length to the floor. Then his muscles tightened and he jerked erect, his eyes opened and blazed into hers with the same cold anger with which he had first greeted her upon entering this room.

"Why?"

"You asked," she countered.

His lids drooped so she could no longer see that icy anger. "So I did. But I did not quite expect to be so quickly served. Now, you have effectively proven your point; three go or none. And it remains to be seen how soon we can find our missing third."

He asked her no more questions and she was glad, since that whirl into nowhere in the abortive attempt at waking had tired her greatly. She moved the stool a little so her back could rest against the wall and she was farther from him. In a little while he got to his feet and paced back and forth as if some driving desire for wider action worked in him to the point where he could not sit still.

Once the door opened, but they were not summoned forth. Instead, food and drink were brought to them by one of the guards; the other stood ready with a crossbow at thigh, his eyes ever upon them.

"We are well served." Hawarel opened the lids of the bowls and inspected their contents. "It would seem we are of importance. Hail, Rugaard, when do we go forth from this room, of which I am growing very tired?"

"Be at peace; you shall have action enough, when the Great One desires it," the officer with the crossbow answered. "The ship from the stars has been sighted; the mountain beacons have blazed twice. They seem to be aiming for the plain beyond Ty-Kry. It is odd that they are so single-minded and come to the same pen to be taken each time. Perhaps Dalskol was right when he said that they do not think for themselves at all, but carry out the orders of an off-world power which does not allow them independent judgment. Your service time will come; and, Mouth of Olava"—he took a step forward to see Tamisan the better—"the Great One says that it might be well to read the sand on your own behalf. False seers are given to those they have belittled in such seeing, to be done with as those they have so shamed may decide."

"As is well known," she answered him. "I have not dealt falsely, as shall be seen at the proper time and in the proper place."

When they were gone she was hungry, and so it seemed was Hawarel, for they divided the food fairly and left nothing in the bowls.

When they were done he said, "Since you are a reader of history and know old customs perhaps you remember one which it is not too pleasant to recall now, that among some races it was the proper thing to dine well as a prisoner about to die."

"You choose a heartening thing to think on."

"No, you chose it, for this is your world; remember that, my dreamer."

Tamisan closed her eyes and leaned her head and shoulders back against the wall. There was a clang of sudden noise, and she gasped out of a doze. The room had grown dark but at the door

was a blaze of light; in that stood the officer, with
a guard of spearmen behind.

"The time has come."

"The wait has been long." Hawarel stood up,
stretched wide his arms as one who has been
ready for too long. Then he turned to her and
once more offered his wrist. She would have
liked to have done without his aid, but she found
herself stiff and cramped enough to be glad of it.

They went on a complicated way through
halls, down stairs until at last they issued out
into the night. Waiting for them was a covered
cart, much larger than the chair on wheels which
had brought her to the castle, with two griffins
between its shafts.

Into this their guard urged them, drawing the
curtains and pegging those down tightly outside, so that even had they wished they could not
have looked out. As the cart creaked out Tamisan
tried to guess by sound where they might be
going.

There was little noise to guide her. It was as if
they now passed through a town deep in
slumber. But in the gloom of the cart she felt
rather than saw movement and then a shoulder
brushed hers and a whisper so faint she had to
strain to hear it was at her ear.

"Out of the castle."

"Where?"

"My guess is the field, the forbidden place."

The memory of the this-world Tamisan
supplied explanation. That was where two other
spacers had planeted, not to rise again. In fact,
the one which had come fifty years ago had

never been dismantled; it stood, a corroded mass of metal, to be a double warning: to the stars not to invade and to Ty-Kry to be alert against such invasion.

It seemed to Tamisan that that ride would never come to an end. Then there was an abrupt halt which bumped her soundly against the side of the cart, and lights bedazzled her eyes as the curtains were pulled aside.

"Come, Champion and Champion-maker!"

Hawarel obeyed first and turned to give her assistance once more, but was elbowed aside as the officer pulled rather than led her into the open. Torches in the hands of spearmen ringed them. Beyond was a colorful mass of people, with a double rank of guards drawn up as a barrier between those and the dark of the land beyond.

"Up there." Hawarel was beside her again.

Tamisan raised eyes. She was almost blinded by the glare as a sudden pillar of fire burst across the night sky. A spacer was riding down on tail rockets to make a fin landing.

V

By the light of those flames, the whole plain was illumined. Beyond stood the hulk of the unfortunate spacer which had last planeted. There, drawn up in lines was a large force of spearmen, crossbowmen, officers with the basket-hilted weapons at their sides. However, as they waited they appeared a guard of honor for the Over-queen, who sat raised above the rest on a very tall chair cart, certainly not an army in battle array.

Those in the ship might well look contemptuously on such archaic weapons as useless. How had those of Ty-Kry taken the other ship and her crew? Was it by wiles and treachery, as the victims might declare, or by clever tricks, as suggested that part of Tamisan who was the Mouth of Olava.

The surface of the ground boiled away under the descent rockets. Then the bright fires vanished, leaving the plain in semi-darkness until their eyes adjusted to the lesser light of the torches.

There was no expression of awe by the waiting crowd. Though they might be, by their trappings, dress and arms, accounted centuries behind the technical knowledge of the newcomers, they were braced by their history to know that they were not to face gods of unknown powers, but mortals with whom they had successfully fought before. *What gives them this attitude toward the star rovers,* Tamisan wondered, *and why are they so adverse to any contact with star civilization? Apparently they are content to stagnate at a level of civilization perhaps five hundred years behind my world. Do they not produce any inquiring minds, any who desire to do things differently?*

The ship was down; it gave no outward sign of life, though Tamisan knew its scanners must be busy feeding back what information they gathered to appear on video-screens. If those had picked up the derelict ship, the newcomers would have so much of a warning. She glanced from the silent bulk of the newly-landed spacer to the Over-queen just in time to see the ruler raise her hand in a gesture. Four men came forward from the ranks of nobles and guards. Unlike the latter they wore no body armor, or helms, but only short tunics of an unrelieved black. In the hands of each was a bow, not the crossbow of the troops, but the yet older bow of expert archers.

That part of Tamisan which was of this world drew a catch of breath, for those bows were unlike any other in the land and those who held them unlike any other archers. It was no wonder ordinary men and women gave them wide room, for they were a monstrous lot. Over the head of each was fitted so skillfully fashioned a mask that it seemed no mask at all, but his natural features, save that the features were not human; the masks were copies of the great heads, one for each point of the compass, which surmounted the defensive walls of Ty-Kry. Neither human nor animal, they were something of both and something beyond both.

The bows they raised were fashioned of human bone and strung with cords woven of human hair. They were the bones and hair of ancient enemies and ancient heroes; the intermingled strength of both were ready to serve the living.

From closed quivers each took a single arrow, and in the torchlight those arrows glittered, seeming to draw and condense radiance until they were shafts of solid light. Fitted to the cords they had a hypnotic effect, holding one's attention to the exclusion of all else. Tamisan was suddenly aware of that and tried to break the attraction, but at that moment the arrows were fired. And her head turned with all the rest in that company to watch the flight of what seemed to be lines of fire across the dark sky, rising up and up until they were well above the dark ship, then following a curve, to plunge out of sight behind it.

Oddly enough, in their passing they had left great arcs of light behind, which did not fade at once, but cast faint gleams on the skin of the ship. It was ingathering one part of Tamisan's mind knew. A laying on of ancient power to influence those in the spacer. That of her which was a dreamer could not readily believe in the efficacy of any such ceremony.

There had been sound with those arrows' passing, a shrill, high whistling which hurt the ears so that those in the throng put hands to the sides of their heads to shut out the screech. A wind arose out of nowhere, with it a loud crackling. Tamisan looked up to see above the Over-queen's head a large bird flapping wings of gold and blue. A closer look revealed it was no giant bird, but rather a banner so fashioned that the wind set it flying to counterfeit live action.

The black-clad archers still stood in a line a little out from the ranks of the guards. Now, though the Over-queen made no visible sign, those about Hawarel and Tamisan urged them forward until they came to front both the archers and the Over-queen's tall throne-cart.

"Well, Champion, is it in your mind to carry

out the duties this busy Mouth has assigned
you?'' There was jeering in the Over-queen's
question, as if she did not honestly believe in
Tamisan's prophecy but was willing to allow a
dupe to march to destruction in his own way.

Hawarel went to one knee but as he did so he
swung his empty sword sheath across his knee,
making very visible the fact that he lacked a
weapon.

"At your desire, Great One, I stand ready. But
is it your will that my battle be without even steel
between me and the enemy?''

Tamisan saw a smile on the lips of the Over-
queen and at that moment glimpsed a little into
this ruler, that it might just please her to will
such a fate on Hawarel. But if the Over-queen
played with that thought for an instant or two,
she put it aside. Now she gestured.

"Give him steel, and let him use it. The Mouth
has said he is the answer to our defense this time.
Is that not so, Mouth?''

The look she gave to Tamisan had a cruel core.

"He has been chosen in the farseeing, and
twice has it read so." Tamisan found the words
to answer in a firm voice, as if what she said was
a decree.

The Over-queen laughed. "Be firm, Mouth;
put your will behind this choice of yours. In fact,
do you go with him, to give him the support of
Olava!''

Hawarel had accepted a sword from the officer
on his left. He rose to his feet and, swinging
the blade, he saluted with a flourish which
suggested that, if he knew he were going to ex-

tinction, he intended to march there as one who moved to trumpet and drums.

"The right be strength to your arm, a shield to your body," intoned the Over-queen. There was that in her voice which one might detect to mean that the words she spoke were only ritual, not intended to encourage this champion.

Hawarel turned to face the silent ship. From the burned and blasted ground about its landing fins arose trails of steam and smoke. The faint arcs left in the air from the arrow flights were gone.

As Hawarel moved forward, Tamisan followed a pace or two behind. If the ship remained closed to them, if no hatch opened, no ramp ran forth, she did not see how they could carry out their plans. If that were so, would the Over-queen expect them to wait hour after hour for some decision from the spacer's commander as to whether or not he would contact them?

Fortunately, the spacecrew were more enterprising. Perhaps the sight of that hulk on the edge of the field had given them the need to learn more. The hatch which opened was not the large entrance hatch, but a smaller door above one of the fins. From it shot a stunner beam.

Luckily it caught its prey, both Hawarel and Tamisan, before they had reached the edge of the sullenly burning turf, so that their suddenly helpless bodies did not fall into the fire. They did not lose consciousness, but only the ability to control slack muscles.

Tamisan had crumpled face down and only the fact that one cheek pressed the earth gave her room to breathe. Her sight was sharply curtailed at the edge of burning grass which crept inexorably towards her. Seeing that she forgot all else.

These moments were the worst she had ever spent. She had conjured up narrow escapes in dreams, but always there had been the knowledge that at the last moment escape was possible. Now there was no escape, only her helpless body and the line of advancing fire.

With the suddenness of a blow, delivering shock through her still painful bruises, she was caught, right side and left, in what felt like giant pincers. As those closed about her body, she was drawn aloft, still face down, the fumes and heat of the burning vegetation choking her. She coughed until the spasms made her sick, spinning in that brutal clutch, being drawn to the spacer.

She came into a burst of dazzling light. Then hands seized her, pulling her down, but holding her upright. The force of the stunner was wearing off; they must have set the beam on lowest power. There was a prickle of feeling returning in her legs and her heavy arms. She was able to lift her head a fraction to see men in space uniforms about her. They wore helmets as if expecting to issue out on a hostile world, and some of them had the visors closed. Two picked her up easily and carried her along, down a corridor, before dropping her without any gentleness in a small cabin with a suspicious likeness to a cell.

Tamisan lay on the floor recovering command of her own body and trying to think ahead. Had they taken Hawarel, too? There was no reason to believe they had not, but he had not been put in this cell. She was able to sit up now, her back supported by the wall, and she smiled shakily at her thought that their brave boast of a championship battle had certainly been brought quickly to naught. It was not that what the Over-queen desired might have run far counter to what happened, but she and Starrex had gained this much of their own objective: they were in the ship she believed also held Kas. Only let the three of them make contact, and they could leave the dream. *And—would our leaving shatter this dream world? How real is it?* She was sure of nothing, and there was no reason to worry over side issues. The time had come to concentrate upon one thing only: Kas.

What should I do? Pound on the door of this cell to demand attention—to speak with the commander of this ship? Would she ask to see all the crew so she could pick out Kas in his this-world masquerade? She had a suspicion that while Hawarel-Starrex had accepted her story, no one else might.

The important thing was some kind of action to get her free and let her search.

The door was opening. Tamisan was startled by what seemed a quick answer to her need.

There was no helmet on the man who stood there, though he wore a tunic bearing the insignia of a higher officer, slightly different from that Tamisan knew from her own Ty-Kry. He also had a stunner aimed at her; at his throat was the box of a vocal interpreter.

"I come in peace."

"With a weapon in hand?" she countered.

He looked surprised; he must have expected a foreign tongue in answer, but she had replied in the Basic which was the second language of all Confederacy planets.

"We have reason to believe that weapons are necessary with your people. I am Glandon Tork of Survey."

"I am Tamisan and a Mouth of Olava." Her hand went to her head and discovered that somehow, in spite of her passage through the air and her entrance into the ship, her crown was still there. Then she pressed the important question:

"Where is the champion?"

"Your companion?" The stunner was no longer centered on her, and his tone had lost some of its belligerency. "He is in safe keeping. But why do you name him champion?"

"Because that is what he is—come to engage your selected champion in right battle."

"I see. And we select a champion in return, is that it? What is right battle?"

She answered his last question first. "If you claim land, you meet the champion of the lordship of that land in right battle."

"But we claim no land," he protested.

"You made claim when you set your fiery ship down on the fields of Ty-Kry."

"Your people then consider our landing a form of invasion? But this can be decided by a single combat between champion? And we pick our man—"

Tamisan interrupted him. "Not so. The Mouth

of Olava selects; or rather the sand selects, the
seeing selects. That is why I have come, though
you did not greet me in honor."

"You select the champion how?"

"As I have said, by the seeing."

"I do not see, but doubtless it will be made
plain in the proper time. And where then is this
combat fought?"

She waved to what she thought was the ship
walls. "Out there on the land being claimed."

"Logical," he conceded. Then he spoke as if to
the air around them. "All that recorded?" Since
the air did not answer him, he was apparently
satisfied by silence.

"This is your custom, Lady—Mouth of Olava.
But since it is not ours, we must discuss it. By
your leave, we shall do so."

"As you wish." She had this much on her side,
he had introduced himself as a member of Survey, which meant that he had been trained in the
necessity of understanding alien folkways. The
simple underlying principle of such training
was, wherever possible, to follow planet cutoms.
If the crew did accept this idea of championship,
then they might also be willing to follow it completely. She could demand to see every member
of the crew and thus find Kas. Once that was
done she could break dream.

But, Tamisan told herself, do not count on too
easy an end to this venture. There was a nagging
little doubt lurking in the back of her mind, and
it had something to do with those death arrows,
and the hulk of the derelict. The people of Ty-
Kry, seemingly so weakly defended, had man-

aged through centuries to keep their world free of spacers. When she tried to plumb the Tamisan-of-this-world's memories as to how that was accomplished she had no answer but what corresponded to magic forces only partly understood. That the shooting of the arrows was the first step in bringing such forces into being she was aware. Beyond that seemed only to lie a belief akin to her Mouth power, and that she did not understand even when she employed it.

She was accepting all of this, Tamisan realized suddenly, as if this world did exist, as if it was not a dream out of her control. Could Starrex's suggestion be the truth, that they had by some means traveled into an alternate world?

Her patience was growing short; she wanted action. Waiting was very difficult. She was sure that scanners of more than one kind were trained on her and she must play the part of a Mouth of Olava, displaying no impatience, only calm confidence in herself and her mission. That she held to as best she could.

Perhaps the time she waited seemed longer than it really was, but Tork returned, to usher her out of the cell and escort her up a ladder from level to level. She found the long skirts of her robe difficult to manage. The cabin they came into was large and well furnished, and there were several men seated there. Tamisan looked from one to another searchingly. She could not tell; she felt none of the uneasiness she had known in the throne room when Hawarel had been there. Of course, that could mean Kas was not one of this group, though a Survey ship did not carry a large crew, mainly specialists of several different callings. There were probably ten, perhaps twenty more than the six before her.

Tork led her to a chair which had some of the attributes of an easirest, molding to her comfort as she settled into it.

"This is Captain Lowald, Medico Thrum, Psycho-Tech Sims and Hist-Techneer El Hamdi." Tork named names and each man acknowledged with a half bow. "I have outlined your proposal to them and they have discussed the matter. By what means will you select a champion from among us?"

She had no sand; for the first time Tamisan realized the handicap. She would have to depend upon touch alone, but somehow she was sure that would reveal Kas to her.

"Let your men come to me, touching hand to mine." She raised hers to lay it, palm up, on the table. "When I clasp that of he whom Olava selects, I shall know it."

"It seems simple enough," the Captain returned. "Let us do as the lady suggests." And he leaned forward to rest his own for a minute on hers. There was no response, nor was there any in the others. The Captain called an order on the intercom and one by one the other members of the crew came to her, touching palm to palm. Tamisan, with mounting uneasiness, began to believe she had erred; perhaps only by the sand could she detect Kas. Though she searched the face of each as he took his seat opposite her and laid his hand on hers, she could see no resemblance to Starrex's cousin, nor was there any inner warning her man was here.

"That was the last," the Captain said as the

final man arose. "Which is our champion?"

"He is not here." She blurted out the truth, her distress breaking through her caution.

"But you have touched hands with every man on board this ship," the Captain answered her. "Or is this some trick—"

He was interrupted by a sound sharp enough to startle. The numbers which spilled from the com by his elbow meant nothing to Tamisan, but brought the rest in that cabin into instant action. A stunner in Tork's hand caught her before she could rise, and once more she was conscious but unable to move. As the other officers pushed through the door on the run, Tork put out his hand, holding her limp body erect in the chair, while with the other he thumped some alarm button set into the table.

His summons was speedily answered by two crewmen who carried her along, to thrust her once more into a cabin. *This is getting to be far too regular a procedure,* Tamisan thought ruefully, as they tossed her negligently on a bunk, hardly pausing to see if she landed safely on its surface or not. Whatever that alert had meant it had certainly once more brought her to the status of prisoner.

Apparently sure of the stunner beam her guard went out, leaving the door open a crack so that she could hear the pad of running feet and the clangs of what could be secondary alarms.

What possible attack could the forces of the Over-queen have launched against a well-armed and already alert spacer? Yet it was plain that those men believed themselves in danger

and were on the defensive. *Starrex—and Kas.
Where is Kas?* The Captain said she had met all
on board. Did that mean that the vision she had
earlier seen was false, that the faceless man in
spacer dress was a creature of her too-active imagination?

*I must not lose confidence. Kas is here—he has
to be!* She lay now trying vainly to guess by the
sounds what was happening. But the first flurry
of noise and movement were stilled, there was
only silence. *Hawarel—where is Hawarel?*

The stunner's power was wearing off. She had
pulled herself up somewhat groggily when the
door of the cabin shot into its wall crack and
Tork and the Captain stood there.

"Mouth of Olava, or whatever you truly are,"
the Captain said, with a chill in his voice which
reminded Tamisan of Hawarel's earlier rage,
"the winning of time may not have been of your
devising—this nonsense of champions and right
battle—or perhaps it was. Your superiors
perhaps deceived you, too. At any rate now it
does not matter. They have done their best to
make us prisoner and will not reply now to our
signals for a parley; so we must use you for our
messenger. Tell your ruler that we hold her
champion and we can readily use him as a key to
open gates shut in our faces. We have weapons
beyond swords and spears, even beyond those
which might not have saved those in that other
ship. She can tie us here for a measure of time,
but we can sever such bonds. We have not come
as invaders, no matter what you believe, nor are
we alone. If our signal does not reach our sister

ship in orbit above, there will be such an ac-
counting as your race has not seen, nor can con-
ceive of. We shall release you now and you shall
tell your Queen this. If she does not send those to
talk with us before the dawn, then it will be the
worse for her. Do you understand?''

"And Hawarel?" Tamisan asked.

"Hawarel?"

"The champion. You will keep him here?"

"As I have said, we have the means to make
him a key for your fortress doors. Tell her that,
Mouth. From what we have read in your champion's mind, you have certain authority here
which ought to impress your Queen."

*Read from Starrex's mind? What do they
mean?* Tamisan was suddenly fearful. *Some
kind of mind probe? But if they did that, then
they must know the rest.* She was utterly con-
fused now, and found it very hard to center her
attention on the matter at hand, that she must
relay this defiant message to the Over-queen.
Since there seemed to be nothing she could do to
protest that action, she would do so. *What reception might I have in Ty-Kry?*—Tamisan shuddered as Tork pulled her from the bunk and half
carried, half led her along.

VI

For the third time Tamisan sat in prison, but
this time she looked not at the smooth walls of a
space ship cabin, but at the ancient stones of the
High Castle ringing her in. Captain Lowald's

estimation of her influence with the Over-queen
had fallen far short, and her plea in favor of a
parley with the spacemen had been overruled at
once. The threat concerning their strange
weapons and their mysterious use of Hawarel as
a "key" was laughed at. The fact that those of
Ty-Kry had successfully dealt with this menace
in the past made them confident that their same
devices would serve as well now. What those
devices were Tamisan had no idea, save that
something had happened to the ship before she
had been unceremoniously bundled out of it.

Hawarel they had kept on board, Kas had disappeared, and until she had both to hand she
was indeed a captive. Kas—her thoughts kept
turning back to the fact that he had not been
among those who had faced her. Lowald had
assured her that she had seen all his crew.

Wait! She set herself to recall his every
word—*what had he said?*—"*You have touched
hand with every man aboard this ship.*" But he
had not said all the crew. *Had there been one
outside the ship?* All she knew of space travel
she had learned from tapes, but those had been
very detailed as they needed to be to supply the
dreamers with factual background and inspira-
tion from which to build fantasy worlds. This
spacer claimed to be a Survey vessel and not
operating alone. *Therefore—it might have a
companion in orbit and there Kas could be.* But,
if that were so, she had no chance of reaching
him.

Now if this were only a true dream . . . Tamisan sighed, leaned her head back against the

dank stone of the wall, and then jerked away
from that support as its chill struck into her
shoulders. *Dreams . . .*

She sat upright, alert and a little excited. *Suppose I could dream within a dream—and find Kas
that way? Is it possible? You cannot tell until
you proved it one way or another.* She had no
stabilizer, no booster, but those were only
needed when a dream was shared. She might
venture as well on her own. *But, if I dreamed
within a dream, can I do aught to set matters
right? Why ask questions I can not answer until
it is put to proof!*

She stretched out on the stones of the cell floor
resolutely blocking off those portions of her
mind which were aware of the present discomfort of her body. Instead, she began the deep,
even breathing of a dreamer, fastened her
thoughts on the pattern of self-hypnosis which
was the door to her dreams. All she had as a goal
was Kas and he as he was in his real person. *So
poor a guide . . .*

She was going under; she could still dream.

Walls built up around her, but these were of a
translucent material through which flowed soft
and pleasing colors. It could not be a space ship.
Then the scene wavered, and swiftly Tamisan
thrust aside that doubt which might puncture
the dream fabric. The walls sharpened and fixed
into a solid state; this was a corridor; facing her
was a door.

She willed to see beyond, and was straightway, after the manner of a proper dream, in that
chamber. Here the walls were hung with the

same sparkling web of stuff which had lined her
chamber in the sky tower. Seeking Kas, she had
returned to her own world. But she held the
dream, curious as to why her aim had brought
her here. Had she been wrong and Kas had never
come with her? If that were so, why had she and
Starrex been marooned in the other dream?

There was no one in the chamber, but she felt a
faint pull drawing her on. She sought Kas; there
was that which promised he was here. There was
a second room; entering, she was startled. This
she knew well: it was the room of a dreamer. Kas
stood by an empty couch, while the other was
occupied.

The dreamer wore a sharing crown, but what
rested on the other couch was not a second
sleeper but a squat box of metal, to which her
dream cords were attached, and Tamisan was
not the dreamer. She had expected to see herself.
Instead, the entranced was one of the locked
minds, the blankness of her countenance unmis-
takable. Dream force was being created here by
an indreamer, and seemingly it was harnessed to
the box.

Given such clues, Tamisan projected the rest.
This was not the same dreaming chamber where
she had fallen asleep; it was a smaller room. Kas
was very much awake, intent upon some dials on
the top of the box. The indreamer and the box,
locked so together, could be holding them in the
other world. *But what of that faint vision of Kas
in uniform? To mislead me? Or is this a misleading dream, dictated by the suspicions I detected
in Starrex concerning his cousin?* This was the

logical reasoning from such suspicions, that she had been sent with Starrex into a dream world and therein locked by an indreamer and machine. *Real, or dream—which?*

Am I now visible to Kas? If this were a dream she should be; if she had come back to reality . . . Her head reeled under the listing of things which might be true, untrue, half true. To prove at least one small fraction, she moved forward and laid her hand on Kas's as he leaned over to make some small adjustment to the box.

He gave a startled exclamation, jerked his hand from under hers and glanced around. But, though he stared straight at her, it was plain he saw nothing; she was as disembodied as a spirit in one of the old tales. *Yet if he has not seen me still he has felt something . . .*

Again he leaned over the box, eyeing it intently as if he thought he must have felt some shock or emanation from it. The dreamer never moved. Save for the slow rise and fall of her breathing, which told Tamisan she was indeed deep in her self-created world, she might have been dead. Her face was very wan and colorless. Seeing that, Tamisan was uneasy. This tool of Kas's had been far too long in an uninterrupted dream. She would have to be awakened if she made no move to break it for herself. One of the dangers of indreaming was this possible loss of the power to break a dream. That occuring, the guardian must break it. Most of dreamers' caps provided the necessary stimuli to do so. But the cap on this dreamer's head had certain modifica-

tions Tamisan had never seen before, and these
might prevent breaking.

What would happen if Tamisan could evoke
waking? Would that also release her and Starrex, wherever he might be, from *their* dream
and return them to the proper world? She was
well drilled in the technique of dream breaking.
Those she had used when she stood in reality
beside a victim who had overstayed the proper
dream time.

She reached out a hand, touched the pulse on
the sleeper's throat and applied slight massage.
But, though her hands seemed corporeal and
solid to her, there was no response in the other.
To prove a point Tamisan aimed a finger, thrusting it deeply as she could into the pillow on
which the dreamer's head rested. Her finger did
not dent that soft roundness, but went into it as if
her flesh and bone had no substance.

There was yet another way; it was harsh and
used only in cases of extremity. But to Tamisan
this could be no else. She put those unsubstan-
tial fingers on the temples of the sleeper, just
below the rim of the dream cap, and concentrated on a single command.

The sleeper stirred, her features convulsed
and a low moan came from her. Kas uttered an
exclamation and hung over his box, his fingers
busy pushing buttons with a care which
suggested he was about a very delicate task.

"*Awake!*" Tamisan commanded with such
force as she could summon.

The sleeper's hands arose very slowly and un-

steadily from her sides and they wavered towards the cap, though her eyelids did not rise.
Her expression was now one of pain. Kas,
breathing hard and fast, kept to his adjustments
on the box.

So they fought their silent battle for possession of the dreamer. Slowly Tamisan was forced
to concede that whatever force lay in that box
overrode all the techniques she knew. But the
longer Kas kept this poor wretch under, the
weaker she would grow. Death would be the
answer, though perhaps that did not trouble
him.

If she could not wake the dreamer and break
the bonds which she was certain now were what
tied her and Starrex to that other world, then she
must somehow get at Kas himself. He had responded to her touch before.

Tamisan slipped away from the head of the
couch and came to stand behind Kas. He
straightened up, a faint relief mirrored on his
face as apparently his box reported that there
was no longer any disturbance.

Now Tamisan raised her hands to either side
of his head, spreading wide her fingers so they
might resemble the covering of a dreamer's cap,
and then brought them swiftly down to cover his
head, putting firm touch on his temples though
she could not exert real pressure there.

He gave a muffled cry, tossed his head from
side to side as if to free himself from a cloud. But
Tamisan, with all the determination of which
she was capable, held fast. She had seen this
done once in the Hive; however, then it had been

used on a docile subject and both the controlled and the dreamer had been on the same plane of existence. Now she could only hope that she could disrupt Kas's train of thought long enough to make him release the dreamer himself. So she brought to bear all her will to that purpose. He was not only shaking his head from side to side now, making it very hard to keep her hands in the proper position, but he was swaying back and forth, his hands up, clawing as if to tear her hold away. It appeared he could not touch her any more than she could lay firm grip on him.

That fund of energy which had enabled her to create strange worlds and hold them for a fellow dreamer was bent to the task of influencing Kas. But, to her dismay, though he ceased his frenzied movements, his clawing for the hands he could not clutch growing feebler, his eyes closed and his face screwed into an expression of horror and rejection of a frightened child. He did not move to the box.

Instead he slumped forward so suddenly that Tamisan was taken wholly unaware, falling half across the divan. In that fall he flailed out with an arm to send the box smashing to the floor, its weight dragging the cap from the dreamer.

She drew several deep breaths, her haggard face now displaying a small trace of returning color. Tamisan, still startled at the results of her efforts to influence Kas, began to wonder if she might have made matters worse. She did not know how much the box had to do with their transportation to the alternate world and whether, if it was broken, they could ever return.

There was one precaution, if she could take it. *If I return to that prison cell in the High Castle—I must, or leave Starrex-Hawarel lost forever—then to leave Kas here, perhaps able again to use his machine—no! But how—since I cannot . . .*

Tamisan looked to the stirring dreamer. The girl was struggling out of the depths of so deep a state of unconsciousness that she was not aware of what lay about her. In this state she might be pliable. Tamisan could only try.

Leaving Kas she went back to the dreamer. Once more touching the girl's forehead, she sought to influence her.

The dreamer sat up with such slow movements of body as one might use were almost unbearable weights fastened to every muscle. In a painfully slow gesture she raised her hands to her head, groping for the cap no longer there. Then she sat, her eyes still shut, while Tamisan drew heavily on her own strength to deliver a final set of orders.

Blindly, for she never opened her eyes, the dreamer felt along the edge of the couch on which she had lain, until her hand swept against the cords which fastened the cap to the box. Her lax fingers fumbled and tightened as she gave a feeble jerk, then another until both cords pulled free. Holding those still in one hand, she slipped from the couch in a forward movement which brought her to her knees, the upper part of her body on the other couch, one cheek touching that of the unconscious Kas.

The strain on Tamisan was very great. She was wavering in her control now, several times those weak hands fell limply as her hold on the dreamer ebbed. But each time she found some small surge of energy which brought them back into action again, so that at last the cap was on Kas, the cords which had connected it to the box in a half coil on which the dreamer's head rested.

So big a chance and with such poor equipment! Tamisan could not be sure of any results, she could only hope. Tamisan released her command of the dreamer who lay against the couch on one side as Kas half lay on the other. She summoned all that she had, all that she sensed she had always possessed, that small difference in dream power she had secretly cherished. Once more she touched the forehead of the sleeping girl and broke her dream within a dream.

It was like climbing a steep hill with an intolerably heavy burden lashed to one's aching back, like being forced to pull the dead weight of another body through a swamp which sucked one down. It was such an effort as she could not endure . . .

Then that weight was gone and the relief of its vanishing was such that Tamisan savored the fact that it did not drag at her. She opened her eyes at last and even that small movement required such an effort that it left her spent.

She was not in the sky tower. These walls were stone, and the light was dusky, coming from a slit high in the opposite wall. She was in the High Castle from which she had dreamed her way back to her own Ty-Kry in a dream within a dream. But how well had she wrought there?

For the present she was too tired to even think connectedly. Bits and pieces of all she had seen and done since she had awakened first in this Ty-Kry floated through her mind, not making any concrete pattern.

It was the mind picture of Hawarel's face as she had seen it last while they marched toward the spacer which roused her from that uncaring drift. She remembered Hawarel and the threat the ship's Captain had made, which the Over-queen had pushed aside. If Tamisan had truly broken the lock Kas had set up to keep them here, then it would be escape. There was no strength in her. She tried to remember the formula for breaking, and knew a stroke of chilling fear when her memory proved faulty. She could not do it now; she must have more time to rest both mind and body. Now she was hungry and thirsty, with such a need for both food and drink that it was a torment. *Do they mean to leave me here without any sustenance?*

Tamisan lay still, listening. Then she inched her head around slowly to view the deeper dusk of her surroundings at floor level. She was not alone.

Kas!

Had she successfully pulled Kas with her? If so, was it that he had no counterpart in this world and so was still his old self?

However, she did not have time to explore that possibility, for there was a loud grating and a line of light marking an opening door. In the beam of a torch stood that same officer who had earlier been her escort. Using her hands to brace

her body, Tamisan raised herself. At the same
time there was a cry from the far corner.

Someone moved there, raised a head and
showed features she had last seen in the sky
tower. It was Kas in his rightful body. He was
scrambling to his feet and the officer and the
guardsman behind him in the doorway stared as
if they could not believe their eyes. Kas shook his
head as if to clear away some mist.

His lips pulled back from his teeth in a terrible
rictus which was no smile. There was a small
laser in his hand. She could not move; he was
going to burn her. In that moment she was so
sure of that she did not even fear, but only waited
for the crisping of her flesh.

But the aim of the weapon raised beyond her
and fastened on the doorway. Under it both officer and guard went down. With one hand on
the wall to steady himself, Kas pulled along until
he came to her. He stood away from the stone,
transferred his laser to the other hand and
reached down to hook fingers in the robe where
it covered her shoulder.

"On—your—feet." He mouthed the words
with difficulty, as if his exhaustion nearly
equaled hers. "I do not know how, or why, or
who. . . ."

The torch, dropped from the charred hand
which had carried it, gave them dim light. Kas
swung her around, thrusting his face very close
to hers. He stared at her intently, as if by the very
force of his glare he could strip aside the mask
her body made for her and force the old Tamisan
into sight.

"You are Tamisan—it can not be otherwise! I do not know how you did this, demon-born." He shook her with a viciousness which struck her painfully against the wall. "Where—is—he?"

All that came from her parched throat were harsh sounds without meaning.

"Never mind." Kas stood straighter now; there was more vigor in his voice. "Where he is—there shall I find him. Nor shall I lose you, demon-born, since you are my way back. And for Lord Starrex, here there will be no guards, no safe shields. Perhaps this is the better way after all. What is this place; answer me!" He slapped her face, his palm bruising her, once more thumping her head back against the wall so that the rim of the Mouth crown bit into her scalp and she cried out in pain.

"Speak! Where is this—?"

"The High Castle of Ty-Kry;" she croaked.

"And what do you in this hole?"

"I am prisoner to the Over-queen."

"Prisoner? What do you mean? You are a dreamer; this is your dream. Why are you a prisoner?"

Tamisan was so shaken she could not marshal words easily, as she had to explain to Starrex. She thought, a little dazedly, that Kas might not accept her explanation anyway.

"Not—wholly—a dream," she got out.

He did not seem surprised. "So the control has that property, has it; to impose a sense of reality." His eyes blazed into hers. "You cannot control this dream, is that it? Again fortune favors me it seems. Where is Starrex now?"

She could give him a truthful answer she was glad, as it seemed to her she could not speak falsely with any hope of belief. It was as if he could see straight into her mind with those demanding eyes of his. "I do not know."

"But he is in this dream somewhere?"

"Yes."

"Then you shall find him for me, Tamisan, and speedily. Do we have to search this High Castle?"

"He was, when I saw him last, outside."

She kept her eyes turned from the door, from what lay there. But he hauled her towards that, and she was afraid she was going to be sick. Where they might be in the interior of the small city which was the High Castle she did not know. Those who had brought her here had not taken her to the core towers, but had turned aside along the first of the gateways and gone down a long flight of stairs. She doubted if they would be able to walk out again as easily as Kas thought to do.

"Come." He pulled at her, dragging her on, kicked aside what lay in the door. She closed her eyes tightly as he brought her past. But the stench of death was so strong that she staggered, retching, with his hand dragging at her, keeping her on her feet and reeling ahead.

Twice she watched glassily as he burned down opposition. His luck at keeping surprise on his side held. They came to the foot of the stairs and climbed. Tamisan held to one hope. Now that she was on her feet and moving, she found a measure of strength returning, so that

she no longer feared falling if Kas released his
hold upon her. When they were out at last in the
night, the damp smell of the underways wafted
away by a rising wind, she felt clean and renewed and was able to think more clearly.

Kas had gotten her this far because of her
weakness, so to his eyes she must continue to
counterfeit that, until she had a chance to act. It
might be that his weapon, so alien to this world
and thus so effective, might well cut their way to
Starrex. That did not mean that once they had
reached him she need obey Kas. She felt that,
face to face with his lord, Kas would be less
confident of success.

It was not a guard that halted them now but a
massive gate. Kas examined the bar and laughed
before he raised the laser and sent a needle-thin
beam to cut as he needed. There was a shout from
above and Kas, almost languidly, swung the
beam to a narrow stair leading from the ram-
parts, laughing again as there came a choked
scream, the sound of a falling body.

"Now." Kas put his shoulder to the gate and it
swung more easily than Tamisan would have
thought possible for its weight. "Where is Starrex? And if you lie—" His smile was threatening.

"There." Tamisan was sure of her direction,
and she pointed to where there was a distant
blaze of torches about the bulk of the grounded
spacer.

VII

"A spacer!" Kas paused.

"Besieged by these people," Tamisan informed him. "And Starrex is a hostage on board, if he still lives. They have threatened to use him in some manner as a weapon and the Overqueen, as far as I know, does not care."

Kas turned on her, his merriment had vanished; his laugh was now a snarl; and he shook her back and forth. "It is your dream; control it!"

For a moment Tamisan hesitated. Should she try to tell him what she believed the truth? Kas and his weapon might be her only hope of reaching Starrex. Could he be persuaded to a frontal attack if he thought that was their only chance of reaching their goal? On the other hand, if she admitted she could not break this dream, he might well burn her down out of hand and take his chances. She thought she had a solution.

"Your meddling has warped the pattern, Lord Kas. I cannot control some elements, nor can I break the dream until I have Lord Starrex with me, since we are pattern-linked in this sequence."

Her steady reply seemed to have some effect on him. Though he gave her one more punishing shake and uttered an obscenity, he looked ahead to the torches and the halfseen bulk of the ship with calculation in his eyes.

They made a lengthy detour away from most of the torches, coming up across the open land to the south of the ship. There was a graying in the sky and a hint that dawn might perhaps be not far away. Now that they could see better, it was apparent that the ship was sealed. No hatch opened on its surface, no ramp ran out. The laser in Kas's hand could not burn their way in, by the method he had opened the gate of the High Castle.

Apparently the same difficulty presented itself to Kas, for he halted her with a jerk while they were still in the shadows, well away from the line of torches forming a square around the ship. Surveying the scene, they sheltered in a small dip in the ground.

The torches were no longer held by men, but had been planted in the ground at regular intervals, and they were as large as outsize candles. The colorful mass which had marked the Overqueen and her courtiers on Tamisan's first visit to the landing field were gone, leaving only a line of guardsmen in a wide encirclement of the sealed ship.

Why did the spacemen not lift and planet elsewhere, Tamisan wondered. Perhaps the confusion in the last moments she had been on board meant that they could not do so. They had spoken then of a sister ship in orbit above. It would seem that had made no move to aid them, though she had no idea how much time had elapsed since last she had been here.

Kas turned on her again. "Can you get a message to Starrex?" he demanded.

"I can try. For what reason?"

"Have him ask for us to come to him." Kas had been silent for a moment before replying. *Is he so* stupid as to believe that I would not give a warning with whatever message I could deliver, or has he precautions against that?

But can I reach Starrex? She had gone into the secondary dream to make contact with Kas. There was no time for such a move now. She could only use the mental technique for inducing a dream and see what happened thereby. She said as much to Kas now, promising no success.

"Be about what you can do now!" he told her roughly.

Tamisan closed her eyes to think of Hawarel as she had seen him last, standing beside her on this very field. She heard a gasp from Kas. Opening her eyes she saw Hawarel, even as he had been then, or rather a pallid copy of him, wavering and indistinct, already beginning to fade, so she spoke in a swift gabble.

"Say we come from the Queen with a message, that we must see the Captain."

The shimmering outline of Hawarel faded into the night. She heard Kas mutter angrily. "What good will that ghost do?"

"I cannot tell. If he returns to that of which he is a part, he can carry the message. For the rest—" Tamisan shrugged. "I have told you this is no dream I can control. Do you think if it were, we two would stand here in this fashion?"

His thin lips parted on one of his mirthless grins.

"You would not, I know, dreamer!"

His head went from left to right as he slowly surveyed the line of planted torches and the men standing on guard between them. "Do we move closer to this ship, expect them to open to us?"

"They used a stunner to take us before," Tamisan warned him. "They might do so again."

"Stunner." He gestured with the laser. Tamisan hoped his answer would not be a headlong attack on the ship with that.

He used it as a pointer to motion her on toward the torch line. "If they do open up," he commented, "I shall be warned."

Tamisan gathered up the long skirt of her robe. It was torn by rough handling, frayed in strips at the hem where she could trip if she caught those rags between her feet. The rough brush growing knee high about them caught at it so that she stumbled now and again, urged on continually by Kas's pulling, when he dug his fingers painfully into her already bruised shoulder.

They reached the torch line. The guards there faced inward to the ship and in this crease of light Tamisan could see that they were all armed with crossbows, not with those of bone which the black-dressed men had earlier worn. Bolts against the might of the ship. The answer seemed laughable, a jesting to delight the simple. Yet the ship lay there and Tamisan could well remember the consternation of those men who had been questioning her within it.

There was a dark spot on the hull of the ship and a hatch suddenly swung open. She recognized it as a battle hatch, though she had only seen those via tapes.

"Kas, they are going to fire." With a laser beam from there they could crisp everything on this field, perhaps clear back to the walls of the High Castle!

She tried to turn in his grasp, to race back and away, knowing already that such a race was lost before she took the first lunging stride. He held her fast.

"No muzzle," he said.

Tamisan strained to see through the flickering light. Perhaps it was a lightening of the sky which made it clear that there was no muzzle projecting to spew a fiery death across them all. But that was a gun port.

As quickly as it had appeared, the opening was closed. The ship was again sealed tightly.

"What?"

Kas answered her half question, "Either they cannot use it, or else they have thought better of doing so—which means, by either count, we have a chance. Now, stay you here! Or else I shall come looking for you in a manner you shall not relish; never fear that I can find you!" Nothing in Tamisan disputed that.

She stood; for after all, apart from Kas's threats, where did she have to go? If she were sighted by any of the guards she might either be returned to prison or dealt with summarily in another fashion. She had to reach Starrex if she were to escape.

She watched Kas make good use of the interest which riveted the eyes of the guards on the ship. He crept, with more ease than she thought possible for one used to the luxury of the sky towers, behind the nearest man.

What weapon he used she could not see; it was not the laser. Instead he straightened to his full height behind the unsuspecting guard, reached out an arm and seemed only to touch the stranger on the neck. Immediately the fellow collapsed without a sound, though Kas caught him before he had fallen to the ground and dragged him backward to the slight depression in the field where Tamisan waited.

"Quick," Kas ordered, "give me his cloak and helm."

He ripped off his own tunic with its extravagantly padded shoulders, while Tamisan knelt to fumble with a great brooch and free the cloak from the guard. Kas snatched it out of her hands, dragged the rest of it loose from under the limp body, and pulled it around him, taking up the helm and settling it on his head with a tap. Then he picked up the crossbow.

"Walk before me," he told Tamisan. "If they have a field scanner on in the ship I want them to see a prisoner under guard. That may bring them to a parley. It is a thin chance, but our best."

He could not guess that it might be a better chance than he hoped, Tamisan knew, since he did not know that she had been once within the ship and the crew might be expecting some such return with a message from the Over-queen. But to walk out boldly past the line of torches— surely Kas's luck would not hold so well; they would be seen by the other guards before they were a quarter of the way to the ship. But she had no other proposal to offer in exchange.

This was no adventure such as she had lived through in dreams. She believed that if she died now she died indeed and would not wake un-

harmed in her own world. Her flesh crawled
with a fear which made her mouth go dry and her
hands quiver as they held wet upon the folds of
her robe. *Any second now—I will feel the impact
of a bolt, hear a shout of discovery, be . . .*

But still Tamisan tottered forward and heard,
with alerted ears, the faint crunch of boots which
was Kas behind her. His contempt for a danger
which was only too real for her, made her wonder, fleetingly, if he did indeed still believe this a
dream she could control, and need not then
watch for any one but her. She could not summon words to tell him of his woeful mistake.

So intent was she upon some attack from behind that she was not really conscious of the ship
towards which they went, until suddenly she
saw another of the ports open and steeled herself
to feel the numbing charge of a stunner.

However, again the attack she feared did not
come. The sky was growing lighter, although
there was no sign of sunrise. Instead, the first
drop of a storm began to fall. Under the
onslaught of moisture from lowering clouds, the
torches hissed and sputtered, finally flickering
out. The gloom was hardly better than twilight.

They came close enough to the ship to board,
when one of the ramps lowered to them, they
stood waiting. Tamisan felt the rise of hysterical
laughter inside her. *What an anti-climax if the
ship refuses to acknowledge us!* They could not
stand here forever and there was no way they
could battle a way inside. Kas's faith in her
communication with the ghost of Hawarel
seemed too high.

But even as she was sure that they faced

failure, there was a sigh of sound from above
them. The port hatch wheeled back into the
envelope of the ship's wall, and a small ramp,
hardly more than a steep ladder, swung creak-
ing out, dropped to hit the charred ground not
far from them.

"Go!" Kas prodded her forward.

With a shrug, Tamisan went. She found it hard
to climb with the heavy, frayed skirts dragging
her back. But by using her hands to pull along
the single rail of the ramp, she made progress.
Why had not the rest of the guards along that
watching line of torches moved? Had it been that
Kas's disguise had indeed deceived them, and
they thought that Tamisan had been sent under
orders to parley a second time with the ship's
people?

She was nearly at the hatch now, could see the
suited men waiting in the shadows above. They
had tanglers ready to fire, prepared to spin the
webs to enmesh them both as easily handled
prisoners. But before those slimy strands
writhed forth to touch (patterned as they were to
seek flesh to anchor) both the waiting spacemen
jerked right and left, clutched with already dead
hands at the breasts of charred tunics from
which arose small, deadly spirals of smoke.

They had expected a guard armed with bow;
they had met Kas's laser, to the same undoing as
the guardsmen at the castle. Kas's shoulder in
the middle of her back sent her sprawling, to
land half over the bodies of the two who had
awaited them.

She heard a scuffle, was kicked and rolled
aside, fighting the folds of her own long skirt,

trying to get out of the confines of the hatch pocket. Somehow, on her hands and knees, she made it forward, since she could not retreat. Now she fetched up against the wall of a corridor and managed to pull around to face the end of the fight.

The two guards lay dead. But Kas held the laser on a third man. Now, without glancing around, he gave an order which she mechanically obeyed.

"The tangler, here!"

Still on her hands and knees, Tamisan crawled far enough back into the hatch compartment to grip one of those weapons. The second she eyed with awakening need for some protection herself, but Kas did not give her time to reach it.

"Give it to me."

Still holding the laser pointed steadily at the middle of the third spaceman, he groped back with his other hand. *I have no choice—no choice—but I do!*

If Kas thinks he has me thoroughly cowed . . . Swinging the tangler around without taking time to aim, Tamisan pressed the firing button.

The lash of the sticky weaving spun through the air, striking the wall, from which it dropped away. Then it struck one arm of the motionless captive, who was still under Kas's threat, and there it clung, across his middle, and on through the air until it caught Kas's gun hand, his middle, his other arm and adhered instantly, tightening with its usual efficiency and tying captor to captive.

Kas struggled against those ever tightening

bands to bring the laser round to bear on Tamisan. Whether he would have used it even in his white-hot rage, she did not know. It was enough that the tangler made sure she could keep from his line of fire. Having ensnared them enough to render them both harmless for a time, Tamisan drew a deep breath and relaxed somewhat.

She had to be sure of Kas. She had loosed the firing button of the tangler as soon as she saw that he could not use his arms. Now she raised the weapon, and with more of a plan, tied his legs firmly together. He kept on his feet, but he was as helpless as if they had used a stunner on him.

Warily she approached him. Guessing her intent, he went into wild wrigglings, trying to bring the adhesive tangler strands in contact with her flesh also. But she stooped and tore at the frayed hem of her robe, ripping up a strip as high as her waist and winding it about her arm and wrist to make sure she could not be entrapped.

In spite of his struggles she managed to get the laser out of his hold, and for the second time knew a surge of great relief. He made no sound, but his eyes were wild and his lips so tightly drawn against his teeth, that a small trickle of spittle oozed from one corner to wet his chin. Looking at him dispassionately, Tamisan thought him nearly insane at that moment.

The crewman was moving. He hitched along as she swung around with the laser as a warning, his shoulders against the wall keeping him firmly on his feet, his unbound legs giving him more mobility, though the cord of the tangler anchored him to Kas. Tamisan glanced around searching for what he appeared desperate to reach. There was a com box.

"Stand where you are!" she ordered.

The threat of the laser kept him frozen. With that still trained on him she darted small glances over her shoulder to the hatch. Sliding along the wall in turn, she managed, the tangler thrust loosely into the front of her belt, to slam the hatch door and give a turn to its locking wheel.

Using the laser as a pointer she motioned him to the com, but the immobile Kas was too much of an anchor. Dared she face the crewman? There was no other way. She motioned with one hand.

"Stand well away."

He had said nothing during their encounter; but he obeyed with an agility which suggested he liked the sight of that weapon in her hand even less than he had liked it when Kas had held it. He stretched to the limit the cord would allow so she was able to burn it through.

Kas spit out a series of obscenities which were only a meaningless noise as far as Tamisan was concerned. Until he was released he was no more now than a well anchored bundle. But the crewman had importance.

Reaching the com before him, she gestured him on to it. She played the best piece she had in this desperate game.

"Where is Hawarel, the native who was brought on board?"

He could lie, of course, and she would not know it. But it seemed he was willing to answer, probably because he thought that the truth would strike her worse than any lie.

"They have him in the lab—conditioning him." He grinned at her with some of the malignancy she had seen in Kas.

She remembered the Captain's earlier threat to make of Hawarel a tool to use against the Overqueen and her forces. Was she too late? There was only one road to take and that was the one she had chosen in those few moments when she had taken up the tangler and used it.

She spoke as she might to one finding it difficult to understand her. "You will call, and you will say that Hawarel will be released and brought here."

"Why?" the crewman returned with visible insolence. "What will you do? Kill me? Perhaps, but that will not defeat the Captain's plans; he will be willing to see half the crew burned—"

"That may be true," she nodded. Not knowing the Captain she could not tell whether or not that was a bluff. "But will his sacrifice save his ship?"

"What can you do?" began the crewman, and then he paused. His grin was gone, now he looked at her speculatively. In her present guise she perhaps did not look formidable enough to threaten the ship, but he could not be sure. One thing she knew from her own time and place: a spaceman learned early to take nothing for granted on a new planet. It might be that she did have command over some unknown force.

"What can I do? There is much." She took quick advantage of that hesitation. "Have you been able to raise the ship?" She plunged on, hoping very desperately that her guess was right. "Have you been able to communicate with your other ship or ships in orbit?"

His expression was her answer, one which fanned her hope into a bright blaze of excitement. The ship *was* grounded, and there was some sort of a hold on it which they had not been able to break.

"The Captain won't listen." He was sullen.

"I think he will. Tell him that we get Hawarel here, and himself, or else we shall truly show you what happened to that derelict across the field."

Kas had fallen silent. He was watching her, not with quite the same wariness of the crewman, but with an emotion she was not able to read. Surprise? Did it mask some sly thought of taking over her bluff, captive though he was?

"Talk!" The need for hurry rode Tamisan now. By this time those above would wonder why their captives had not been brought before them. Also, outside, the Over-queen's men would certainly have reported that Tamisan and a guard had entered the ship; from both sides enemies might be closing in.

"I cannot set the com," her prisoner answered.

"Tell me then."

"The red button."

But she thought she had seen a slight shift in his eyes. Tamisan raised her hand, to press the green button instead. Without accusing him of the treachery she was sure he had tried, she said again more fiercely,

"Talk!"

"Sannard here." He put his lips close to the com. "They, they have me; Rooso and Cambre are dead. They want the native—"

"In good condition," hissed Tamisan, "and now!"

"They want him now, in good condition," Sannard repeated. "They threaten the ship."

There came no acknowledgment from the com in return. Had she indeed pressed the wrong button because she was overly suspicious? What was going to happen? She could not wait.

"Sannard." The voice from the com was metallic, without human inflection or tone.

"Sir?"

But Tamisan gave the crewman a push which sent him sliding back along the wall until he bumped into Kas and the bonds of both men immediately united to make them one struggling package. Tamisan spoke into the com.

"Captain, I do not play any game. Send me your prisoner or look upon that derelict you see and say to yourself, 'that will be my ship.' For this is so, as true as I stand here now, with your man as my captive. Send Hawarel alone, and pray to whatever immortal powers you recognize that he can so come! Time grows very short and there is that which will act if you do not, to a purpose you shall not relish!"

The crewman, whose legs were still free, was trying to kick away from Kas. But his struggles instead sent them both to the floor in a heaving tangle. Tamisan's hand dropped to her side as she leaned against the wall, breathing heavily.

With all her will she wanted to control action as
she did in a dream, but only fate did that now.

VIII

Though she sagged against the wall Tamisan
felt rigid, as if she were in a great encasement of
su-steel. As time moved at so slow a pace as not
to be measured normally, that prisoning hold on
her body and spirit grew. The crewman and Kas
had ceased their struggles. She could not see the
crewman's face, but that which Kas turned to her
had a queer, distorted look. It was as if before her
eyes, though not through any skill of hers, he
was indeed changing and taking on the aspect of
another man. Since her return to the sky tower in
the second dream, she had known he was to be
feared. In spite of the fact that his body was
securely imprisoned, she found herself edging
away, as if by the very intentness of that hostile
state he could aim a weapon to bring her down.
But he said nothing and lay as broodingly quiet
and impassive as though he had foreknowledge
of utter failure for her.

She knew so little, Tamisan thought, she who
had always taken pride in her learning, in the
wealth of lore she had drawn upon to furnish her
memory for action dreaming. The spacecrew
might have some way of flooding this short corridor with a noxious gas, or using a hidden ray
linked with a scanner to finish them. Tamisan
found herself running her hands along the walls

and studying the unbroken surface a little wildly, striving to find where death might enter
quietly and unseen.

There was another bulkhead door at the end of
the short corridor; at a few paces away from the
outer hatch a ladder ascended to a closed trap.
Her head turned constantly from one of those
entrances to the other, until she regained a
firmer control of herself. *They have only to wait
to call my bluff—only to wait . . .*

Yes! They have waited and they are . . .

The air about her was changing; there was a
growing scent in it. It was not unpleasant, but
even a fine perfume would have seemed a stench
when it reached her nostrils under present con-
ditions. The light which radiated from the
juncture of the corridor roof and ceiling was
altering. It had been that of a moderately sunlit
day; now it was bluish. Under it her own brown
skin took on an eerie look. *I have lost my throw!
Maybe, if I could open the hatch again, let in the
outer air . . .*

Tamisan tottered to the hatch, gripped the
locking wheel and brought her strength to bear.
Kas was writhing again, trying to break loose
from his unwilling partner. Oddly enough, the
crewman lay limp, his head rolling when Kas's
heaving disturbed his body, but his eyes were
closed. At the same time Tamisan, braced
against the wall, her full strength turned on the
need for opening the door, knew a flash of surprise. Was it her over-vivid imagination alone
which made her believe that she was in danger?
When she rested for a moment and drew a deep
breath . . .

In her startlement she could have cried out aloud; she did utter a small sound. She was gaining strength, not losing it. She breathed in every lungful of that scented air, and she was breathing deeper and more slowly, as if her body desired such nourishment. It was a re-storative.

Kas, too? She turned to glance at him again. Where she breathed deeply, with lessening ap-prehension, he was gasping, his face ghastly in the change of light. Then, even as she watched, his struggles ended and his head fell back so that he lay as inert as the crewman he sprawled across.

Whatever change was in progress here af-fected Kas and the crewman, the latter faster than the former, but not her. Now her trained imagination took another leap. Perhaps she had not been so far wrong in threatening those on this ship with danger. Though she had no guess as to how it was done, this could be another strange weapon in the armament of the Over-queen.

Hawarel? The spacemen had probably never intended to send him. *Dare I go to seek him?* Tamisan wavered, one hand on the hatch wheel, looking to the ladder and the other door. If all within this ship had reacted to the strange air, there would be none to stop her. If she fled the ship she would face the loss of the keys to her own world and might be met by some evil fate at the hands of the Over-queen. She had broken prison, and she had left dead men behind her. As the Mouth of Olava she shuddered from the judgment which would be rendered one

deemed to have practiced wrongful supernatural acts.

Resolutely Tamisan went to the door at the
end of the corridor. It was true that she had no
choice at all. She must find Starrex and somehow bring him here, so that they three could be
together. They must win a small space of time in
which to arrange a dream breaking, or she was
totally defeated.

She loosened her belt a little so she could draw
up her robe through it, shortening its length and
leaving her legs freer. There was the tangler and
Kas's laser. In addition, there was the mounting
feeling of strength and well being, though an
inner warning suggested she beware of over-
confidence.

The door gave under her push and she looked
out upon a scene which first startled and then
reassured her. There were crewmen in the corridor. But they lay prone as if they had been
caught while on their way to the hatch. Lasers (a
slightly different pattern than that Kas had
brought) had fallen from their hands, and three
of the four wore tanglers.

Tamisan picked her way carefully around
them, gathering up all the weapons in a fold of
her robe, as if she were some maiden in a field
plucking an armful of spring flowers. The men
were alive, she saw as she stooped closer, but
they breathed evenly as if peacefully asleep.

She took one of the tanglers, discarding the
one she had used, fearing its charge might be
near exhaustion. As for the rest of the collection,
she dropped them at the far end of the passage-

way and turned the beam of Kas's weapon on
them, so she left behind a metal mass of no use
to anyone.

Her idea of the geography of the ship was
scanty. She would simply have to explore and
keep exploring until she found Starrex. She
would start at the top and work down. She found
a level ladder and three times came upon sleeping crewmen. Each time she made sure they
were disarmed before she left them.

The blue shade of light was growing deeper,
giving a very weird cast to the faces of the sleepers. Making sure her robe was tightly kilted up,
Tamisan began to climb. She had reached the
third level when she heard a sound, the first she
had noted in this too silent ship since she had
left the hatchway.

She stopped to listen, deciding it came from
somewhere in the level into which she had just
climbed. With laser in hand she tried to use it as
a guide, though it was misleading—and might
have come from any one of the cabins. Each door
she passed Tamisan pushed upon. There were
more sleepers: some stretched in bunks, others
on the floors, seated at tables with their heads
lying on them. But she did not halt now to collect
weapons; the need to be about her task, free of
this ship, built in her as sharp as might a slaver's
lash laid across her shrinking shoulders.

Suddenly the sound grew louder as she came
to a last door and pushed it. Now she looked into
a cabin not meant for living but perhaps for a
kind of death. Two men in plain tunics were
crumpled by the threshold as if they had had

some limited warning of danger to come and had tried to flee and fell before they could reach the corridor. Behind them was a table and on that a body, very much alive, struggled with dogged determination against confining straps.

Though his long hair had been clipped and the stubble of it shaven to expose the full nakedness of his entire scalp, there was no mistaking Hawarel. He not only fought against the clamps and straps which held him to the table, but in addition he jerked his head with sharp, short pulls, to dislodge disks fastened to his forehead, which were connected to a vast box of a machine which filled one quarter of the cabin.

Tamisan stepped over the inert men, reached the side of the table, and jerked the disks away from the prisoner's head; perhaps his determined struggles had already loosened them somewhat. His mouth had opened and shut as she came to him as if he were forming words she could not hear, or could not voice. But as the apparatus came away in her hands he gave a cry of triumph.

"Get me loose!" he commanded. She was already examining the underpart of the table for the locking mechanism of the straps and clamps. It was only seconds before she was able to obey his order.

Bare to the waist, he sat upright, and she saw beneath, where his shoulders and the upper part of his spine had rested on the table, a complicated series of disks.

"Ah." Before she could move, he scooped up the laser she had laid on the edge of the table when she had freed him. The gesture he made with it might not have been only to indicate the door and the need for hurry, but perhaps also was a warning that with a weapon in his hands he now thought he was in command of the situation.

"They sleep everywhere," she told him. "And Kas—he is a prisoner—"

"I thought you could not find him; he was not one of the crew."

"He was not. But I have him now, and, with him, we can return."

"How long will it take?" Starrex was down on one knee, searching the two men on the floor. "What preparation will you need?"

"I cannot tell." She gave him the truth. "But—how long will these sleep? Their unconsciousness is, I think, some trick of the Overqueen's."

"It came unexpectedly for them," Starrex agreed. "And you may be right that this is only preliminary to taking over the ship. I have learned this much: their instruments and much of their equipment has been affected so they cannot trust them." Hawarel's face was grim under its bluish, deadman's coloring. "Otherwise, I would not have survived this long as myself."

"Let us go!" Now that she had miraculously (or so it seemed to her) succeeded, Tamisan was even more uneasy, wanting nothing to spoil their escape.

They found their way back to the corridor before the hatch while the ship still slept. Starrex knelt by Kas and then looked with astonishment at Tamisan. "But this is the real Kas!"

"It is Kas, real enough," she agreed. "And there is a reason for that. But need we discuss it now? If the Over-queen's men come to take this ship—I tell you her greeting to us may be worse than any you have met here. I remember enough of the Tamisan who is the Mouth of Olava to know that."

He nodded. "Can you break dream now?"

She looked around her a little wildly. *Concentration—no, somehow I can not think so clearly.* It was as if the exultation the fumes of that scented air had awakened in her was draining. With that sapping went what she needed most.

"I—I fear not."

"It is simple then." He stopped again to examine the tangle cords. "We shall have to go to where you can." She saw him set the laser on its lowest beam and burn through the cords which united Kas to the crewman, though he did not free his cousin from the rest of his bonds.

But what if we march out of the hatch into a waiting party of the Over-queen's guards? They had the tangler, the laser, and perhaps the half-smile of fortune on their side. They would have to risk it.

Tamisan opened the inner door of the pressure chamber. The dead men lay there as they had fallen, and fighting nausea, she dragged one aside to make room for Starrex, who carried Kas over his shoulder, moving slowly under that burden. There was a fold of cloak wrapped about the prisoner to prevent any contact between the cords and Starrex's own flesh. The outer hatch was open.

A blast of icy rain, with the added bite of the wind which drove it, struck violently at them. It had been dawn when Tamisan had entered the ship, but outside now the day was no lighter; the torches had been extinguished. Tamisan could see no lights, as, shielding her eyes against the wind and rain, she tried to make out the line of guards.

Perhaps the severe weather had driven them all away. She was sure no one waited at the foot of the ramp, unless they were under the fins of the ship, sheltering there. That chance they would have to take. She said as much and Starrex nodded.

"Where do we go?"

"Anywhere away from the city. Give me but a little shelter and time . . ."

"Vermer's Hand over us and we can do it," he returned. "Here, take this!"

He kicked an object across the metal plates of the deck and she saw it was one of the lasers used by the crewmen. She picked it up in one hand, the tangler in the other. Burdened as he was by Kas, Starrex could not lead the way. She must now play in real life such an action role as she had many times dreamed. But this held no amusement, only a wish to scuttle quickly into any form of safety wind and rain would allow her.

The ramp being at a steep angle, she feared slipping on it, and had to belt the tangler, hold on grimly with one hand and moving much more slowly than her fast-beating heart demanded. She was anxious that Starrex in turn might lose footing and slam into her, carrying them both to disaster.

The strength of the storm was such that it was a battle to gain step after step even though she reached the ground without mishap. Tamisan was not sure in which direction she must go to avoid the castle and the city. Her memory seemed befuddled by the storm and she could only guess. Also, she was afraid of losing contact with Starrex, for, as slowly as she went, he dragged even more behind.

Then she stumbled against an upright stake, and putting out her hand, fumbled along it enough to know that this was one of the rain quenched torches. It heartened her a little to learn that they had reached the barrier and that no guards stood there. Perhaps the storm was a lifesaver for the three of them.

Tamisan lingered, waiting for Starrex to catch up. Now he caught at the torch, steadying himself as if he needed that support.

His voice came in wind-deadened gusts; it was labored. "I may have in this Hawarel a good body, but I am not a heavy-duty android. We must find your shelter before I prove that."

There was a dark shadow to her left, it could be a coppice. Even trees or tall brush could give them some measure of relief.

"Over there." She pointed, but did not know if, in this gloom, he could see.

"Yes." He straightened a little under the bur-

den of Kas and staggered in the direction of the
shadow.

They had to beat their way into the vegetation.
Tamisan, having two arms free, broke the path
for Starrex. She might have used the laser to cut,
but the ever-present fear that they might need
the charges for future protection kept her from a
waste of their slender resources.

At last, at the cost of branch-whipped and
thorn-ripped weals in their flesh, they came into
a space which was a little more open. Starrex
allowed his burden to fall to the ground.

"Can you break dream now?" He squatted
down beside Kas, as she dropped to sit panting
near him.

"I can—"

But she got no farther. There was a sound
which cut through even the tumult of the storm,
and that part of them which was allied to this
world knew it for what it was, the warning of a
hunt. Since they *were* able to hear it, they must
be the hunted.

"The Itter hounds!" He put their peril into
words.

"And they run for us!" Mouth of Olava or not,
when the Itter hounds coursed on one's track
there was no defense, for they could not be controlled once they were loosed to chase.

"We can fight them."

"Do not be too sure of that," he answered. "We
have the lasers, weapons not of this world. The
weapon which put the ship's crew to sleep did
not vanquish us; so might an off-world weapon
react the other way here."

"But Kas—" she thought she had had found a weak point in his reasoning, much as she wanted to believe he had guessed rightly.

"Kas is in his own form, which is perhaps more akin to the crewmen now than to us. And, by the way, how is it that he is?"

She kept her tale terse, but told him of her dream within a dream and how she had found Kas. She heard him laugh.

"I was right then in thinking my dear cousin might well be at the center of this web. However, now he is as completely enmeshed as the rest of us. As a fellow victim, he may be more cooperative."

"Entirely so, my noble lord." The voice out of the dark between them was composed.

"You are awake then, cousin. Well, we would be even more awake. There is a struggle here in progress between two sets of enemies who are both willing to make us a third. We had better travel swiftly elsewhere if we would save our skins. What of it, Tamisan?"

"I must have time."

"What I can do to buy it for you, I will." That carried the force of a sworn oath. "If the lasers act outside the laws of this world, it may be that they can even stop the Itter hounds. But get to it!"

She had no proper conductor, nothing but her will and the need. Putting out her hands she touched the bare, wet flesh of Starrex's shoulder, but was more cautious in seeking a hold on Kas, lest she encounter one of the tangle cords. Then she exerted her full will and looked far in, not out.

It was no use; her craft failed her. There was a momentary sensation of suspension between two worlds. Then she was back in the dark brush where the growing walls did not hold off the rain.

"I cannot break the dream. There is no energy machine to step up the power." But she did not add that perhaps she might have done it for herself alone.

Kas laughed then. "It would seem my sealer still works in spite of all your meddling, Tamisan. I fear, my noble lord, you will have to prove the effectiveness of your weapons after all. Though you might set me free and give me arms, necessity making allies of us after all."

"Tamisan!" Starrex's voice was one to bring her out of the dull anguish of her failure. "This dream—remember, it may not be a usual dream after all. Could another world door be opened?"

"Which world?" At that moment her memories of reading and viewing tapes were a whirl in her head. The voiceless call of the Itter hounds to which this Tamisan was attuned made her whole body cringe and shiver and addled her thinking even more.

"Which world? Any one—think, girl, think! Take a single change, if you must, but think!"

"I cannot. The hounds—aheeee—they come —they come! We are meat for the fangs of those who course the dark runnels under moonless skies. We are lost." The Tamisan who dreamed slipped into the Mouth of Olava, and the Mouth of Olava vanished in turn, and she was only a naked, defenseless thing crouching under the shadow of a death against which she could raise no shield. She was—

Her head rocked, the flesh of her cheeks stung as she swayed from the slaps dealt her by Starrex.

"You are a dreamer!" His voice was imperative. "Dream now then as you have never dreamed before, for there is that in you which can do this, if you will it."

It was like the action of that strange-scented air in the ship; her will was reborn, her mind steadied. Tamisan the dreamer pushed out that other, weak Tamisan. *But what world? A point—give me but a decision point in history!*

"Yaaaah—" the cry from Starrex's throat was not now meant to arouse her. Perhaps it was the battle challenge of Hawarel.

There was a pallid snout about which hung a dreadful sickening phosphorescence, thrust through the screen of brush. She sensed rather than saw Starrex fire the laser at it.

A decision—water beating in on me. Wind rising as if to claw us out of the poor refuge to be easy meat for the hunter. Drowning—sea—sea—the Sea Kings of Nath!

Feverishly she seized upon that. She knew little of the Sea Kings who had once held the lace of islands east of Ty-Kry. They had threatened Ty-Kry itself so long ago that that war was legend, not true history. And they had been tricked, their king and his war chiefs taken by treachery.

The Ill Cup of Nath. Tamisan forced herself to remember, to hold on that. And, with her choice made, again her mind steadied. She threw out

her hands, once more touching Starrex and Kas,
though she did not choose the latter, her hand
went without her conscious bidding as if he
must be included or all would fail.

The Ill Cup of Nath—this time it would not be
drunk!

Tamisan opened her eyes. *Tamisan—no—I am
Tam-sin!* She sat up and looked about her. Soft
coverings of pale green fell away from her bare
body. And, inspecting that same body, she saw
that her skin was no longer warmly brown; instead it was a pearl white. What she sat within
was a bed fashioned in the form of a great shell,
the other half of it arching overhead to form a
canopy.

Also, she was not alone. Cautiously she turned
somewhat to survey her sleeping companion.
His head was a little hidden from her so that she
could see only a curve of shoulder as pale as her
own and hair curled in a tight-fitting cap, the
red-brown shade of storm-tossed seaweed.

Very warily, she put out a finger tip, touched it
to his hunched shoulder, and knew! He sighed
and began to roll over toward her. Tamisan
smiled and clasped her arms under her small,
high breasts.

She was Tam-sin, and this was Kilwar, who
had been Starrex and Hawarel, but was now Lord
of LockNer of the Nearer Sea. But there had been
a third! Her smile faded as memory sharpened.
Kas! Anxiously she looked about the room, its
nacre-coated walls, its pale green hangings, all
familiar to Tam-sin.

There was no Kas, which did not mean that he

might not be lurking somewhere about, a disruptive factor if his nature held true.

A warm arm swung up about her waist. Startled, she looked down into sea-green eyes, eyes which knew her and which also knew that other Tamisan. Below those very knowledgeable eyes, lips smiled.

His voice was familiar and yet strange, "I think that this is going to be a very interesting dream, my Tam-sin."

She allowed herself to be drawn down beside him. Perhaps, no, surely he was right.

ANDRE NORTON, a prolific writer who modestly describes herself as "rather a staid teller of old-fashioned stories," has had a varied career that included years as a librarian, at the Library of Congress, and as manager of her own bookstore.

Since emerging in the 1950's as a writer of first-rate science fiction and fantasy, she has written over 80 books. Her *Witch World* series has become a science fantasy classic. In 1977 Andre Norton was awarded the prestigious Gandalf Award for life achievement in fantasy writing at the World Science Fiction Convention.

ANDRE NORTON now lives in Florida, in the company of her many feline associates.

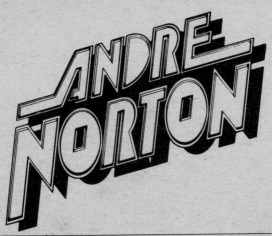

ANDRE NORTON

☐ 78746-0	**STORM OVER WARLOCK**	$2.50
☐ 78435-6	**THE STARS ARE OURS**	$2.50
☐ 86610-7	**VOORLOPER**	$2.75
☐ 89706-1	**WITCH WORLD**	$2.50
☐ 87877-6	**WITCH WORLD #2:** **WEB OF THE WITCH WORLD**	$2.50
☐ 66836-4	**PLAGUE SHIP**	$2.25
☐ 07899-0	**BREED TO COME**	$2.50
☐ 75835-5	**SECRET OF THE LOST RACE**	$2.25
☐ 82347-5	**TREY OF SWORDS**	$2.50
☐ 74986-0	**SARGASSO OF SPACE**	$2.50
☐ 22377-X	**EYE OF THE MONSTER**	$2.50
☐ 43676-5	**KEY OUT OF TIME**	$2.50

Prices may be slightly higher in Canada.

Available at your local bookstore or return this form to:

ACE SCIENCE FICTION
Book Mailing Service
P.O. Box 690, Rockville Centre, NY 11571

Please send me the titles checked above. I enclose _____. Include 75¢ for postage
and handling if one book is ordered; 25¢ per book for two or more not to exceed
$1.75. California, Illinois, New York and Tennessee residents please add sales tax.

NAME_____

ADDRESS_____

CITY_____ STATE/ZIP_____

(allow six weeks for delivery.)   **SF12**

Science Fiction
From
Marion Zimmer Bradley

☐ 07180-5	**THE BRASS DRAGON**	$2.25
☐ 15935-4	**DOOR THROUGH SPACE**	$1.95
☐ 20668-9	**ENDLESS UNIVERSE**	$2.95
☐ 79113-1	**SURVEY SHIP**	$2.75

THE DARKOVER SERIES

☐ 06857-X	**THE BLOODY SUN**	$2.95
☐ 77953-0	**STAR OF DANGER**	$2.50
☐ 89255-8	**THE WINDS OF DARKOVER**	$2.50
☐ 91175-7	**THE WORLD WRECKERS**	$2.50

Available at your local bookstore or return this form to:

ACE SCIENCE FICTION
Book Mailing Service
P.O. Box 690, Rockville Centre, NY 11571

Please send me the titles checked above. I enclose _____ Include 75¢ for postage and handling if one book is ordered; 25¢ per book for two or more not to exceed $1.75. California, Illinois, New York and Tennessee residents please add sales tax.

NAME_____

ADDRESS_____

CITY_____STATE/ZIP_____

(allow six weeks for delivery)

SF11

MAGICQUEST

Dear Fantasy Reader,
Ace Books has brought you the best
in adult fantasy for over thirty years.
Now we are pleased to offer the very
best in young adult fantasy, under
our MagicQuest logo. MagicQuest
brings classic and popular works of
YA fantasy into paperback for fantasy
readers and collectors of all ages.

___ 80839-5/$2.25 **THE THROME OF THE ERRIL OF SHERILL**
Patricia A. McKillip

The Throme of Erril of Sherill, a book of songs more beautiful than
the stars themselves does not exist. But if the Cnite Caerles is to
win the sad-eyed daughter of the King of Everywhere, he must find
it, and so he sets out on an impossible quest...
Illustrated by Judith Mitchell. By the World Fantasy Award-winning
author of *The Forgotten Beasts of Eld* and *The Riddle-Master Trilogy*.

___ 65956-X/$2.25 **THE PERILOUS GARD**, *Elizabeth Marie Pope*

Based loosely on the ballad *Tam Lin*, this is the tale of a young man
in bondage to the Queen of the Fairies, and a young woman who
ventures deep into the fairy realms to win him back again...
Newberry Honor Winner and ALA Notable Book.

___ 03115-3/$2.25 **THE ASH STAFF**, *Paul R. Fisher*

Mole is the oldest of six orphans raised by an old sorcerer in the
magical land of Mon Ceth. When their protector dies, Mole must take
up his staff and become the leader of the orphan band. As they leave
the safety of their mountain, little do they know that the are about
to plunge headlong into war. First in the popular *Ash Staff* series.

___ 82630-X/$2.25 **TULKU**, *Peter Dickinson*

Peter Dickinson is best known to fantasy readers for *The Blue Hawk* —
and for *Tulku,* a splendid tale of a young American boy in 19th century
China who travels to the myth-ridden mountains of Tibet — where
the magic is real. An ALA Notable Book.

___ 16621-0/$2.25 **THE DRAGON HOARD**, *Tanith Lee*

Lee has been called "The Princess of Royal Heroic Fantasy" by
The Village Voice — but before she became a bestselling adult writer
Ms. Lee had already made a name for herself with several tales
of YA fantasy adventure. Wacky, wonderful and thoroughly magical,
Ms. Lee's YA fiction is available in paperback for the first time.

Prices may be slightly higher in Canada.

Available at your local bookstore or return this form to:

TEMPO
Book Mailing Service
P.O. Box 690, Rockville Centre, NY 11571

Please send me the titles checked above. I enclose _____ Include 75¢ for postage
and handling if one book is ordered; 25¢ per book for two or more not to exceed
$1.75. California, Illinois, New York and Tennessee residents please add sales tax.

NAME _____

ADDRESS _____

CITY _____ STATE/ZIP_____

(Allow six weeks for delivery.)   **T-15**